Robert's Rules of Ordure

Adam,
Remember when we bought <u>Robert's Rules of Order</u>? That was terrific.

Happy Birthday

Shannon

Rebert's Rules of Ordure

a guidebook to the social and political language of our times

J L McClellan

Writer's Showcase
San Jose New York Lincoln Shanghai

Rebert's Rules of Ordure
a guidebook to the social and political language of our times

All Rights Reserved © 2000 by J L McClellan

No part of this book may be reproduced or transmitted in any form or by any means, graphic, electronic, or mechanical, including photocopying, recording, taping, or by any information storage retrieval system, without the permission in writing from the publisher.

Writer's Showcase
an imprint of iUniverse.com, Inc.

For information address:
iUniverse.com, Inc.
5220 S 16th, Ste. 200
Lincoln, NE 68512
www.iuniverse.com

ISBN: 0-595-15860-9

Printed in the United States of America

Preface

This work began as a release for the outrage I felt listening to political and social propaganda in the public arena. Its form, content and intent were strongly influenced the original *The Devil's Dictionary* by Ambrose Bierce.

I have made a serious effort not to use direct quotations without attribution and I believe I have been successful—when I have deliberately drawn from the writing or utterances of others, I have paraphrased, *pro* or *contra* the original usage, depending on the original meaning and my mood. If I have erred, it is probably because something resonated so well in my mind that I learned it without ever realizing where it came from.

The exception to this rule is my use of elements from dictionary definitions, especially to highlight incongruous multiple meanings to the same word, or, in a couple of instances, to bring useful or interesting terms to a broader attention.

In this context, I must express my appreciation to the G. & C. Merriam company for their *New International Dictionary of the English Language*, in both First and Second Editions, and to the Funk & Wagnalls Company for their *New Practical Standard Dictionary of the English Language*.

A

Abacus: n.:
Chinese slide rule; the second pocket calculator, the first having been a set of fingers; the origin of digital mathematics.

Abase: v.t.:
prepare oneself for a meeting with one's employer, legislator or mother-in-law.

Abdication: n.:
formal declaration of a sovereign of his assessment of his fitness to rule.

Ability: n.:
the difference between those who collect accomplishments in their lives and the rest of us, who merely dream of them.

Abnormal: adj.:
different from me; not in accordance with my tastes, whims or prejudices. Always be careful to observe the distinction between abnormal and unusual.

Abortion: n.:
heiring-out the recreation room.

The issue of the legality and availability of medical abortion has become the most divisive issue in Christianity since the Reformation. Americans align themselves with the Right-to-Life and the Right-to-Liberty camps and freely apply the old maxim "all's fair in love and war." The methods used show clearly that they're not in love.

Above the law: phrase:
descriptive of any member of the White House staff (especially in "law-and-order" administrations.)

Abscond: v.i.:
exercise power of attorney.

Absence: n.:
the primordial love philtre; anodyne to many a troubled marriage.

Absent: adj.:
1) subject of gossip.
2) about to be selected as head of an unpopular committee.

Absinthe: n.:
a legendary liqueur that actually had the kind of effects on its consumers that the temperance movement attribute to all kinds of liquor.
Fosterer of alcoholic amory; it is celebrated in the saying "Absinthe makes the heart grow fonder."

Absolutely: adv.:
approximately.

Absolutism: n.:
the stance we take to disguise the fact that we're not confident enough of our beliefs to let them stand on their own.

Absurd: adj.:
different from my beliefs.

Abuse: n.:
any pattern of use that I don't approve of; an excuse for hysteria and overreaction.
Various kinds of abuse exist in culture, and some constitute real social problems. The standard reaction of hysterically criminalizing any activity that has elements in common with the abuse, however, rarely accomplishes anything positive toward reducing the problem.

Academe: n.:
fabulous land where the towers are of ivory and the seats are upholstered with sheepskin.

Academic: adj.:
isolated from the real world; irrelevant.

Academic freedom: n.:
an institution that allows professors to teach what is, instead of what is popular; the only barrier that prvents all science being political science.

Accessible: adj.:
1) (of a public official) having a fixed price list.
2) (of a building) altered at great expense to inconvenience the hale.
3) (of art) vapid or vulgar.

Accordion: n.:
a musical instrument whose behavior in use emulates the patterns of traffic flow during rush hour.

Accountant: n.:
one who, when asked "how much is 2+2 ?" replies "How much do you need it to be?"

Acephalous: adj.:
in the fashion of Irving's Horseman, any of several of Henry VIII's ex-wives, or one of Ko-Ko's clients.

Acerbic: adj.:
   the condition of a stable Bosnia.

Acerebral: adj.:
   Intellectual, as contrasted with cerebral: intellectual.

ACLU: acronym:
   Activists Caring Little for Us. To conservatives, the Atheist Communist Lawyers' Union.

Acme: n.:
   a minority-owned mail-order company in the Southwest, noted for the unvarying quality of its products; patronized by genius coyotes.

Act: v.i.:
   to tell something that is not true, without lying.

Action: n.:
   the seldom peaceful refuge for those who lack adequate facility at planning; the quietly effective result for those who have no such lack.

Activist: n.:
   professional or semi-pro axe-grinder.
   Someone who has found a way to get air time without having to accomplish anything worthwhile or newsworthy.

Activity: n.:
   mindless substitute for reason or discourse.

Actor: n.:
   one who disproves the common wisdom that "you can't lie with body language."

Actuary: n.:
   oddsmaker. Specifically, one who works for the house in the insurance gamble. It's his job to make sure the house doesn't lose.

Acupuncture: n.:
   the art of getting needled by your doctor, and liking it.

Acute: adj.:
of me, sharp; of you, pointed; of him, narrow.

Ad infinitum: imported phrase:
1) duration of PBS pledge week.
2) home shopping channel.

Ad nauseam: n. phrase:
1) constipation, diarrhea or dyspepsia ads run at meal time.
2) reaction to political campaign ads.

Adage: n.:
predigested wisdom. Frequently beginning "Confucius say…"

Adam: proper name:
the probable original author of most of your favorite jokes.

Addictive: adj.:
a medical property defined by legal declaration or political expediency, so that marijuana and cocaine are addictive, while nicotine and caffeine are not.

Additive: n.:
in prepared foods, a substance used for the purpose of making us insensitive to deficiencies of quality.

Adapt: v.t.:
to modify beyond recognition, while retaining the original name.

Adept: adj.:
not visibly clumsy.

Admit: v.t.:
let in, especially against one's will, as the rest of the camel into the tent, following its nose.

When a lawyer gets someone to admit something, he considers he has won a victory.

Theater and other tickets say "Admit one." Considering the size of the bribe it took to get in, they must *really* not want you there.

Adolescence: n.:
a phase of life wherein the denizens have two primary goals:

1) to be seen as adults

2) to unmercifully irritate those who are already recognized as adults.

Adolescent: n.:
once, an apprentice adult; now, a child with hormones and an attitude. A male whose eye holds that beauty is in a D-cup.

Adopt: v.t.:
to take as one's own the finished product, without having had to do the work of creation; as Congress adopting the report of a committee. Steal.

Adult: n.:
the mechanism used by reproductive cells to generate more reproductive cells.

Adulterate: v.t.:
to take one's youth, especially another's.

Adulteress: n.:
technical term for a woman who has chosen to act like a man in the arena of marriage observances.

Adultery: n.:
an activity in which adults revel as much as the infants do in their infantry.

Originally, a woman had to be married to participate, but modern liberalization of language has made it accessible to nonmarried women as well.

Adversity: n.:
a tribulation easy to endure, so long as it's someone else's.

Advice and consent: n.phrase:
nitpicking and obstructionism.

Affectation: n.:
the artificial foundation on which society develops its height.

Affection: n.:
the warmth of emotion, in which we may bask. One of those few things in life of which we have more, the more we give away.

Affirmative Action: n.:
the Government visiting the sins of the fathers upon the children.

Affluenza: n.:
the disease of conspicuous consumption.

Aftershock: n.:
credit card statement. The sequel to sticker shock.

Agape: n.:
the emotion of the slack-jawed.

Age of Reason: n.:
middle age. The stage between Youth, when you know everything, and Old Age, when you know what you know, and nobody can tell you any different.

Ageism: n.:
1) the belief that age confers wisdom and that youth implies impetuosity and irresponsibility.
2) the belief that youth confers vigor and enthusiasm and that age imposes a burden.

Aggressive: adj.:
pushy. Of the type, "give him an inch and he thinks he's a ruler."

Agnostic: n.:
one who does not claim to have all the answers to religious questions, therefore not a religious person.

Agony: n.:
misery unyoked.

Air Traffic Control: n.:
official Nintendo. A government-issue game of chance.

Airhead: n.:
target for paratroopers.

Alacrity: n.:
the calm, measured response of a sitting legislator to a solicitation by moneyed interests or populous pressure groups.

Alkali: n.:
salt with the tang taken out of it.

Alkaloid: n.:
one of a family of compounds developed by plants to kill insects and give a buzz to people. Several are addictive psychoactive substances, such as nicotine, caffeine, cocaine.

"All the news that's fit to print": motto:
all the news that fits the publisher's prejudices.

"All's fair in love and war": motto:
a misrepresentation promulgated primarily by those who are adept at neither.

Alien: n.:
one from a different time or clime. Generally depicted as being avaricious and voracious (ask Sigourney Weaver), the same attributes we are drawn to in our leaders but recoil from in our neighbors.

Alleged: n.:
a magic word sprinkled freely throughout news reports of crimes and suspects of crimes; intended to ward against libel suits.
Since most newswriters have no idea what the word means, it is used improperly and inaccurately more often than not.
For the record, alleged means stated without proof.

Allegory: n.:
a description of one thing in the guise of another, such as the same old stuff in a new package; kind of like a fable, but without the moral implications.

Alone: adj.:
in the best of company—or the worst.

Alpaca: n.:
the animal which supplies the wool from which the best Republican cloth coats are woven.

Altar: n.:
an impediment that bears the same relation to the chapel as the TV set to the living room.

Altruism: n.:
self-aggrandizement. A transaction wherein the profits are not declared.

Amaze: v.t.:
stimulate incompleteness of understanding and insufficiency of imagination.

Ambiguous: adj.:
in the fashion of the phrasing of those rules which purport to restrict the actions of Business or Government or of the indiviual operatives therein.

Ambition: n.:
that element of reach that allows it to exceed our grasp: what a Heaven's for. Ambition is traditionally undeterred by reality.

America First: motto:
(working) Americans last.

The American Dream: n.:
something for nothing (or, more properly, next to nothing.)
The bulk of immigrants came to the New World to see the streets that were "paved with gold," where a man could become wealthy without having to work all his life for someone else. The promise was empty, but the only ones who found that out were the ones who had believed it in the first place.

The American People: n.:
that portion of the population that agrees with my positions.

Amerind: n.:
acronym for American Indigene.
One whose family came to the land when immigration laws were a lot stricter than they are now and were enforced by Nature, not by politically malleable bureaucrats.
Activists hold the position that the land the US took from them at the point of a sword is rightfully theirs because their ancestors had to fight to wrest it from the inferior peoples who had been wasting its bounty before those ancestors arrived.

Ammunition: n.:
game counters for playing to determine whose side God is really on.

Amnesty: n.:
a declaration by government that there are too many prisoners to fit in the jails, just now.

Amnesty International: n.:
a short-sighted organization who wilfully confuse our just protection of society from dangerous malefactors with our opponents' malicious persecution of guiltless dissidents.

Amoral: adj.:
having the audacity to ignore my value system.

Amputation: n.:
surgical downsizing.

Anal retentive: n.:

1) a personality type characterized by a strong attention to detail and form.

2) a person demonstrating the reference personality type. Given what the anus generally retains, we can begin to understand the general reaction to such people.

Anal-retentive: adj.:
having the character of the personality type called anal retentive.
[Note] this pair of definitions is intended to answer the question "Is anal retentive spelled with or without a hyphen?" The short answer is, of course, "Yes." The proper answer is "It depends." This is, of course, unacceptable to anyone who would ask the question.

Analyst: n.:
one who charges doctor's rates to sit and listen for a short hour at a time. Derived from anal, the region where the average analyst seems to have his head.

Anarchy: n.:
conservative's characterization of liberal democracy.
Anarchy is the most advanced form of government, as it requires total involvement and responsibility of its citizens. No culture has successfully implemented an anarchy; all attempts have quickly degenerated to bossism or some form of feudalism.

Idealistic and naive students keep trying, however, aided and abetted by nihilists and damnfools and, of course, the everpresent Media.

Anathema: proper name:
daughter of Zeus; patron deity of the party out of power.

Anatomy: n.:
something we all have, but it looks better on girls.

Ancient: adj.:
older than my parents.

"And a little child shall lead them": phrase:
these days, it's more likely just to be someone who acts like one.

Androgyne: n.:
Attic Greek foreshadow of Michael Jackson.

Android: adj.:
shaped like Andrew.

Angel: n.:
someone on my side.

Anhedonist: n.:
one who cannot experience pleasure; rare.
Not to be confused with Antihedonist: one who cannot bear anyone else experiencing pleasure; common.

Animal husbandry: n.:
traditional coursework at land-grant colleges.

Animal magnetism: n.:
that power that causes pet hair to stick to your clothes. In magnetism, opposites attract, which explains why white dog hair is drawn to your best blue serge, while linen has an affinity for black fur.

Animal Rights: n.:
an oxymoronic movement which must be viewed as the inevitable consequence of the stuffed-animal toy industry and the commercial, if not artistic, success of Disney movies.
The movement as currently espoused shows a profound lack of understanding of either rights or animals.

Anodyne: n.:
surcease from sorrow, or from pain.
The aspiration of many a political speech; oft promised, ne'er delivered.

Anomie: n.:
the social state toward which modern urban culture naturally gravitates, as it has been doing at least since the time of Socrates:
Our youth now love luxury. They have bad manners, contempt for authority; they show disrespect for their elders and love chatter in place of exercise; they no longer rise when elders enter the room; they contradict their parents, chatter before company; gobble up their food and tyrannize their teachers.
Most readers consider the remarks contemporary.

Anonymous: adj.:
afraid or ashamed to admit to one's writings.
  proper name:
the most prolific author in recorded history.

Anorexia: proper name:
a minor Roman deity, goddess of weight control

Answering machine: n.:
the method that allows modern business to thrive on impersonal contact.

Antibiotic: n.:
a chemical that kills bacteria slightly faster than it kills patients.

AntiChrist: n.:
during the Middle Ages, the Pope, according to the Pope.

Antipathy: n.:
ashes of the flames of passion.

Apartheid: n.:
a system of racial oppression so abhorrent that members of the oppressed races migrated toward it at the rate of tens of thousands per year for most of the years is was in effect.

Aphorism: n.:
archaic term for a sound bite.

Aphrodisiac: n.:
the Holy Grail of steroid research; an agent which either creates desire in another to match the appetites of the wielder or engenders ability to match the desires of the user.
The ultimate power over members of the appropriate sex.

Apollonian: adj.:
the kind of pleasure that does not involve getting falling-down drunk and rolling around in the mud; much denigrated by those whose pleasures consist of getting drunk and falling down in the mud.

Apologist: n.:
spokesperson for the other side.

Appeal: n.:
juridical expression of contempt of (a lower) court.
beggary in formal dress.

Applejack: n.:
a potation derived from apples, which has about the same effects as a blackjack.
a portmanteau word containing "apple brandy" and "blackjack" in combined reference to cause and effect.

Appropriation: n.:
a legislative promise to make the taxpayer pay.

Approval: n.:
recognition of benefit.

April Fool: proper name:
cultural icon, companion to the March Hare. The two are icons of the Easter season, the holiest of times to orthodox Christians.

Aquarius: n.:
astrological sign and age, popularized in the 60s. We are now in the Middle Age of Aquarius.

Arbeit macht frei: imported phrase:
German for workfare.

Arbitrator: n.:
mediator of differences between individuals or groups. In this day and age, most commonly hired from Samuel Colt, Smith and Wesson, or one of their collegial agencies.

Archaic: adj.:
of my parents' generation or, inconceivably, earlier.

Archeology: n.:
the science that divines a culture's religion by sifting through its garbage pits.

Arguable: adj.:
not yet ruled on by the Supreme Court.

Argument: n.:
an attempt to change through the use of words the nature of a reality that others have created through their actions.

Aria: n.:
what the fat lady sings to signal that it's over.

Army: n.:
an entity that marches on its belly—or slithers, or whatever that verb of locomotion happens to be.
alternatively, **Armey.**

Arrest: v.t.:
in the eyes of the court, accuse; in the eyes of the press, convict.

Arrogant: adj.:
unable, or simply unwilling, to recognize my obvious superiority.

Ars gratia artis: imported phrase:
"Art for the gratification of the Artist."
When paired with the image of a roaring lion, "Art for the gratification of the bank account."

Ars longa, vita brevis: imported phrase:
motto of the legend-in-his-own-mind artist, who is convinced that decadent modern times don't appreciate his genius. Tragically, art critics foster and foment this self-delusion.

Art: n.:
a product or event produced by someone identifying themselves as an artist, especially if endorsed by a collector, critic or gallery.
Traditionally, imitation life.

Artesia: proper name:
Roman goddess of broken water mains.

Artful: adj.:
full of art; dishonest.

Article: n.:
a part of speech that comes in two flavors—definite and indefinite. English is unusual in having both kinds, which can be a source of great confusion: someone who has found *a* truth is tempted to believe he has discovered *the* truth. Such a belief is rarely justified.

Articulate: adj.:
glib.

Artificial horizon: n.:
a device the pilot keeps in the cockpit to remind him which way is up.

Artificial intelligence: n.:
1) buzzword used to overawe those who suffer a deficiency of the natural kind.
2) made-up spy reports. See *Our Man In Havana*, or anything declassified by the CIA.

Artificial respiration: n.:
breathing for people whose health is not good enough to support the authentic kind.

Asinine: adj.:
exhibiting the perspicacity, wisdom and relevance of a public figure, especially a political figure.

Ask to resign: v.t.:
fire ceremoniously.

Asp: n.:
Cleopatra's experimental livng bra; a real killer of a lingerie project.

Aspersions: n.:
1) slanders or scandals; frequently confused with aspirations.
2) baptisms, especially by sprinkling.

Aspirations: n.:
dreams beyond one's station, i.e., impediments to success and satisfaction.

Ass: n.:
one whose views are opposed to mine.

Assassin: n.:
a dissident who has decided to enhance the impact of his individual vote.

Assassinate: v.t.:
bring about the death of a public figure I approve of.

Assassination: n.:
the delicate care with which we nurture the reputation of our opponents during the campaign season.

Assertiveness training: n.:
socially sanctioned training for bad manners: acceptable largely for its expense, which qualifies it as a status symbol.

Assisted suicide: n.:
the outcome of pointing a gun at police officers; a method of steadily increasing popularity. Nearly all other forms, involving members of other professions, are illegal.

Astrology: n.:
secular religion of the New Age; the belief that those little lights in the sky that you can't even make out through the light pollution of the city, minutely control the intimate details of your life.

Astronomical: adj.:
too many to envision, as the number of stars in the sky or the number of relatives on a Congressman's staff.

Astronomer: n.:
one who makes his life observing the private and public lives of the stars; not to be confused with the paparazzi, who makes his living peering into the private lives of stars.

At sixes and sevens: phrase:
low, down. The origins of the reference are obscure in the age of digital clocks.

Atom: n.:
indivisible boogie man of the Twentieth Century.

Atone: v.i.:
attempt to make a right by committing a second wrong.

Atheist: n.:
one to whom Nothing is sacred.
one who has a religious faith in the absence of any Deity.

Athletic scholarship: n.:
license for illiteracy.

Attention span: n.:
1) the length of time something is featured in the news.
2) the interval before the next commercial.

Austere: adj.:
exhibiting the warmth and fashionability of an eremite monk.

Austerity program: n.:
economic social engineering so severe that officials are sometimes obliged to accept a reduction in their income from bribes.

Authentic: adj.:
1) real, genuine.
2) having the appearance, but not the actuality, of being real or genuine.

In which way shall we speak now of an Authentic American Hero?

Author: n.:
one who has discovered how to don the mantle of omnipotence.

Authority: n.:
1) armaments, and the battalions to wield them.
2) reputation.

Authorities come in three grades:

a) eminent: having the status to impede progress in their own field;

b) prominent: having the status to impede progress in related fields, as well as his own;

c) pre-eminent: having enough status in the media to get his prejudices in the way of progress culture-wide.

Autocratic: adj.:
in the fashion of a badly spoiled child.

Automaton: n.:
mechanical dittohead.

Automobile: n.:
the device which stands as master of the average modern household. Literally, self-mover, which name superceded all the others based on the observation of the device in its natural environment, where it proceeds apparently without consciousness or intelligent direction.

Automobilia: proper name:
a strange land whose history runs complementary to that of America—for example, in Automobilia, Lincoln is the rich man's Ford. In either, though, a "better idea" is one that assures more income for the auto makers.

Autonomy: n.:
the fruit of Tantalus, as translated into the language of modern civic government.

Avant-garde: adj.:
artsy-fartsy; usually, with the intent to shock or offend. The term is frequently used to disguise inadequate vision and poor execution.

Avarice: n.:
"He who dies with the most toys, wins."
There used to be a literary device of referring to "wealth beyond your dreams of avarice." Dreamers are much more adept now.

Awkward: adj.:
   possessing a level of grace and coordination less than me at my best.

B

Babble: v.i.:
   speak on the floor of the House.

Babel: proper name:
   site of the original cocktail party.

Backstab: v.t.:
   prepare for advancement within or into executive ranks.

Backward nation: n.:
   one which has not yet elected to take significant portions of its arable land and convert them to golf courses.

Bad: adj.:
   1) I don't like it.
   2) disobedient.
   3) good. Freud would have been proud…

Bad rap: n. phrase:
   an old bit of underworld jargon upgraded to the status of tautology by a host of hip-hoppers.

"Badges? We don't need no stinking badges.": quote:
   motto of the no-knock narcs.
Bail: n.:
   (refundable) price of your "get out of jail" card.
Bailey: adj.:
   pertaining to getting criminals released by the expenditure of money.
      n.:
   the most popular variety of Beetle.
Baksheesh: n.:
   a user fee extracted at the point of use by the appropriate governing official. Often misunderstood by Westerners and misinterpreted as graft.
Balanced budget: n.:
   a result that everyone desires so long as it's balanced on someone else's back; a budget with equal amounts of pork allocated to the Left and the Right.
Balanced Budget Amendment: n.:
   the ultimate expression of the debunked belief that it is possible to instill discipline by legislative fiat; sort of a shot of anabolic steroids for the body politic. One is somehow reminded of those Swiss monkey-gland clinics.
Bald: adj.:
   inclined to complain about kids' wearing their hair too long.
Bald Men's Association: n.:
   the "Just say no to rugs" organization.
Balderdash: n.:
   criticism, by a stranger.
Ball: n.:
   a formal party.

v.i.:
have an intimate, informal party.

Ballot: n.:
pacifier to the body politic.

Ballroom: adj.:
a style of dancing which requires that trousers not be excessively tight.

Balls: n.:
equipment necessary for participation in most outdoor sports.

Ban: v.t.:
encourage; as the Congress, the rights of the citizen.

Banana: acronym:
Build Almost Nothing Anywhere Near Anything; the imago of the Nimby, frequently aged by fermentation with *Saccharomyces cerevisiae*, especially the Chardonnay variety.

Band-aid: n.:

1) a method for quickly and superficially treating a symptom while leaving the underlying problem to take care of itself.

2) a cosmetic fix or coverup.

The term is derived from a registered trade name of a product that did its job so well that consumers couldn't think of any other term to use to refer to its competitors.

Bandwagon: n.:
would-be juggernaut; usually powered by attachment to the coattails of a popular candidate; generally quick in the mud.

Bar: n.:
a fixture over which justice is dispensed—or liquor.

Barleycorn, John: proper name:
an avatar of Demon Rum. Friend of Jim Beam, Jack Daniels, and some foreign guy named Johnnie Walker.

Barratry: n.:
the fancy legal word for ambulance chasing. See any plane crash, train wreck or chemical spill.
For several months Bhopal, India was the barratry capitol of the world.
Barratry is nominally illegal in many jurisdictions, but the laws are not enforced for fear of causing collapse in the markets for BMWs, 4-wheel-drive sport-utility vehicles and time-share condominiums.

Basque: n.:
a language too difficult for even the Devil to learn, sort of like C++, only with rhymes and useful nouns.

Bawdy: adj.:
of, or pertaining to, the natural functioning of the homonymous "body."

Bear: n.:
large, aggressive, rapacious omnivore; metaphor for those who believe that the stock market will crash.
    v.t.:
to carry, especially an overwhelming or insupportable burden, such as the cross that the Christian right have deeded to us.

Bear market: n.:
Wall Street activity which tends to create among Streeters the demeanor of its namesake.

Beautiful People: n.:
people with money whom the reporter wants to suck up to.

Beauty: n.:
a property which things I like have and things I dislike lack.

Bebop: n.:
the first major non-Classical form to set musicality ahead of the music.

Beef: n.:
complaint, grievance.
A veiled reference to the quality of cowmeat served in, especially fast-food, restaurants.

Beefeater: proper name:
a British endangered species.

Beelzebub: proper(?) name:
ancient holder of the title "Lord of the Flies." More recently this title would have devolved on Levi Strauss and most recently on Calvin Klein.

Beer: n.:
Mankind's oldest synthetic medicine; amber bonding agent; elixir of conquest; quicker icebreaker.

Beetle: n.:
1) appropriate nickname for a lawyer:
   a) has a hard shell, making it harder to squash than other crawlers-under-rocks;
   b) to pound until finished;
   c) to frown or scowl ominously, especially in an attempt to intimidate.
2) the insect responsible for preventing the army ants from taking over the world.

(Apologies to Mort Walker.)

Beginning of the end: phrase:
end of the beginning.

Behave rationally: v. phrase:
   act as I would wish you to.

Behaviorist: n.:
   member of psycho-cult whose members are not more complex in action or motivation than pigeons. In the Nature vs. Nurture conflict, the ultimate Nurturist, which is ironic in consideration of the paucity of nurturing in their child rearing principles.

Belief: n.:
   a drug self-administered to dull the critical faculties.

Beltway: n.:
   a barrier drawn to separate the interests of the elected from those of the electorate.
   Those who work inside the beltway are so out of touch that they consider leaving office to work in their law firms to be getting back to the real world.

Benedictine: n.:
   a marvelous potion which explains the ability of the monastic followers of St Benedict to maintain their vows through those cold medieval winters.

Best: adj.:
   my favorite.

Bias: n.:
   a characteristic of any reportage that does not show my side in its best light.

Bidet: n.:
   a piece of Continental porcelain that has sown confusion and dismay throughout ranks of American tourists.

Big: adj.:
   good.

Bigger: adj.:
  better.

Biggest: adj.:
  "New and Improved."

Bigot: n.:
  one who dislikes groups that I support.

Bilingual education: n.:
  a system that ensures that the student is unlikely to become fluent in either of two languages.

Bill of Rights: n.:
  an obsolescent addendum to the Constitution, originally placed there by a bunch of radicals who did not believe in the infallibility of either elected or appointed officials, or of their hirelings.
  Of the original 10 articles, only one is currently observed without significant qualification: the Third.

Biotechnology: n.:
  engineering with a life of its own.

Birdbrained: adj.:
  having an intellectual capacity limited to finding meals and mates and to seeing how much noise one can make; qualified to be a legislator or a lawyer; marginally qualified to be a rock star or talk-show host.

Bishop: n.:
  a shepherd whose flock consists of shepherds.

Bismarck: proper name:
  historical patron of the culinary arts, after whom were named a herring and a jelly donut.

Bitch: n.:
  demeaning term for a woman who behaves in ways of which I do not approve, *e.g.*, belongs to the wrong political party.

Euphemized as "sounds-like-witch."
> v.i.:

converse in the traditional fashion of American underlings when speaking of their positions and/or of their (organizational) superiors.

"Bite the Bullet": v phrase:

go through an experience that really tightens your jaws.

Commonly used these days in business management, where it refers to budget reductions: the bullets you are to bite are delivered from the muzzle of a gun.

Bitter: adj.:

sour.

Black: adj.:

1) (British usage) not European.
2) of the color of night, hence fearsome, unlucky, covert; e.g., young black male, Black Friday, blackout.

Blame: v.t.:

assign guilt, responsibility or liability.

Conservatives like to blame everyone outside their clique for whatever they dislike; liberals believe that no individual should ever be blamed, but only groups.

> n.:

the fuel with which politics, religion and the law are powered.

Blamethrower: n.:

favorite weapon of the guilty and the shameful.

Bland: adj.:

having the character of institutional food: spiceless, salt-free and lacking anything to get your teeth into and enjoy. Like primetime television programming; or the politically correct version of a textbook.

Blandishment: n.:

political promise from the Left.

Blank verse: n.:
bland poetry. A form much affected by poets who lack the vocabulary to find rhymes, or the rhythm to identify meter.

Blasé: adj.:
having developed calluses on the organs of delight.

Blasphemous: adj.:
contrary to my beliefs.

Bleak: adj.:
with all the warm colors bleached out.

Blind: adj.:
Showing the penetrating visual acuity of a bar panel overseeing the professional behavior of its member attorneys.

Blind trust: n.:
An instrument we require of our politicos who own stock; and attitude our politicos require of those of us who don't own enough stock.

Block: v.t.:
obstruct; as block grants to the states to support social programs.

Blockbuster: n.:
1) the realtor who places the first ethnic family into a white neighborhood.
2) a show that the critic liked and that filled the house for at least two performances.

Blue: adj.:
1) the color that a person turns on being deprived of air or warmth.
2) the traditional color of conservatism, as blue-pencil for censorship, bluenose for prudery, bluestocking for Puritan.

"Hurrah for the red, white and blue." (-necked, lily-and-nosed)

3) the color that provides illumination without warmth.

Blue law: n.:
imposition of the religious institution of Sunday Sabbath on everyone else at the point of a (policeman's) gun. A classic example of the traditional implementation of the principle of separation of church and state. One of the "traditional values that made our nation great."

Blue-collar: adj.:
of a class of jobs that put dirt under the fingernails.
The way to tell the difference between a blue-collar job and a white-collar job is to note the bathroom procedure:
a white-collar worker goes into the bathroom, does his business, washes his hands and goes back to work; a blue-collar worker goes into the bathroom, washes his hands, does his business and goes back to work.

Blue-sky: adj.:
referring to an improbable dream.
The term evolved in the environment of the modern city.

Bluenose: n.:
one whose attitude is so lofty as to impede their oxygen supply.

Boarding house: n.:
a place where he who hesitates is last.

Boat: n.:
a ship with low self-esteem.

Body language: n.:
quiet eloquence.
Many people think it's impossible to lie in body language; these people have never watched an actor or actress at work.

Bon mot: n.:
what a snob thinks his sophomoric sarcasm is.

Boo: n.:

1) a word used by adults or older children to elicit fright reactions from small children.

2) a word used by hemp users to elicit childish rage reactions from conservatives.

Boob tube: n.:

a traditional term which has taken on a whole new meaning with the advent of T & A programming. Especially note the soaps, teenage dance programs, beauty pageants and the Spanish language channels.

Book: n.:

source of misinformation with higher status than a magazine or newspaper, but less than a journal. The brick from which libraries are assembled.

Boolean: adj.:

the kind of logic which is used by engineers to manufacture computers. Not to be confused with the logic used by lawyers to make fortunes: Bull-ean; or that used by governments to make policy: Bully-an.

Boom: v.i.:

what bulls do in the market.

Boomer: n.:

fallout from the Population Explosion.

Boorish: adj.:

exhibiting the same social characteristics as my opponent.

Bootstrap: n.:

self-activating lifting device.

v.t.:
start (or, much more often, restart) a computer; from "boot", collegiate slang for "vomit", referring to the reaction elicited by the computer's habit of crashing.

Born again: adj phrase:
demonstrating "born yesterday" acuity.

Bottom line: n.:
locus of an MBA's head.

Bounty hunter: n.:
privatised policeman.

Bowdlerization: n.:
the low-salt version of a literary work.

Brandy: n.:
the refined and condensed soul of the grape.

Bread: n.:
1) the staff of life;
2) money.

Break even: v.i.:
snap, leaving a smooth, sharp cutting edge.

Brevity: n.:
the key ingredient of a successful speech (rare).

Bribe: n.:
rental of a public official.
v.t.:
lubricate the machinery of government, especially in petroleum rich countries.

Bridge: n.:
1) an important source of secular zealotry.

2) a structure intended to compensate for toothlessness; cf. Bridge to the 21st Century.

Brigand: n.:
occupant of the brig.

Bright: adj.:
casting enough light for me to be able to discern my reflection.

Brilliant: adj.:
euphemism for mediocre. Commonly used in reference to one's children, or, more frequently, grandchildren. Occasionally used to refer to the boss's ideas.

Brotherly love: n.:
an Old Testament principle, lavishly illustrated with the images of such paragons as Cain and Abel, or Joseph and his brothers.
The proof of the value of such tales is to be seen to this day in such enlightened precincts as Ireland or Lebanon, or around black Christian churches all over the South.

Buchanan: proper name:
1) a President of the Nineteenth Century
2) a presidential candidate for the Nineteenth Century.

"The Buck stops here": motto:
truth in government. Unfortunately, the meaning of 'buck' has changed since Harry Truman's time. Now, it's thousands of bucks; inflation, you know.

Budget: n.:
the map we use to plot the course of our journey into debt.
    v.i.:
do without.

Budget analyst: n.:
an important functionary in Business and Government, named in recognition of tthe source of his numbers.

Bug: v.t.:

1) irritate

2) spy on

the culmination of this duality came with the Nixon tapes.

    n.:

distasteful occupant of baseboards, back yards and computer programs. Especially prevalent in the latter, where the commonality has led to a new name for the species: "feature."

Bulimia: proper name:
minor goddess, patron(ess) of weight loss programs.

Bull: n.:
a half-word, applied most often to whips and people who think the stock market will go up.

Bull market: n.:
Wall Street activity, the touting of which should provide copious organic mulch for one's rose garden (which the Street, of course, never promised you.)
The usage reflects the similarities between Wall Street and other markets, such as the neighborhood china shop.

Bullrush: n.:

1) a word which, mistaken as a phrase, sums up a modern media career.

2) reinforcement for dittoheads.

Bully: n.:
a term which has evolved from an adjective denoting great import, to a noun indicating a person of great self-importance, or any entity that behaves equally badly.
an individual who behaves as though he thinks himself a government.

Bully pulpit: n.:
any podium, when used by bullies.

Bumblebee: n.:
a housefly designed to MIL-specs.

Bunko: n.:
confidence game; swindle. From the Spanish word for "bank." Perhaps the Savings and Loan is not as modern an institution as we thought.

Bunraku: n.:
Japanese puppetry with no strings attached. Limited to the theater and having no applicability to the Diet.

Burma-Shave: proper name:
the most prolific and successful publisher of popular rhyme during the mid part of the Twentieth Century.

Burp: n.:
onomatopoetic eructation.

Burro: n.:
an ass named for a hole in the ground.

Bus: n.:
1) politically correct transportation that spews toxic pollution of its own and engenders more from the cars it obstructs in the daily commutes; the most flexible impediment of mass transit.

2) a group of signal paths in a computer that have a similar effect on the computer signals that the transit vehicle has on commuters.
   v.t.:
to dislocate children and neighborhoods in the name of political correctness; to dramatically increase the cost per student of public education, especially in times of voter revolt and tightened budgets; to commit a second wrong on the children in an attempt to right a prior wrong against the parents.

Business: n.:
commercial intercourse.

Business as usual: phrase:
give the voters the business; give business the voters—on a platter.

Business of Government: n.:
government of the people, by the bureaus, for the businesses.

Buss: n.:
a friendly, if somewhat ostentatious, gesture between two people, involving the mouth of one person and whatever portion of the anatomy is convenient of the other.

Bust: n.:
1) image of the head and neck, with a suggestion of the shoulders.
2) the breast, or in certain periods, the breasts.
3) an arrest.
4) total collapse; complement of boom; the favorite food of Wall Street bears.

Butt: n.:
cigarette.
So called for its cleanliness and delicate aroma.

Butter: n.:
   a substance valued traditional lie detector: it wouldn't melt in your mouth, if you were a politician, salesman or other professional liar.

Butterfly: n.:
   Nature's ongoing lesson in balance. In spite of the great damage their caterpillars do, is there anyone who would do away with butterflies?

Buzzword: n.:
   camouflage language.
   Used to disguise the fact that either you don't know what you're talking about or what you're saying doesn't mean anything.

Byssus: n.:
   the mechanism through which a mussel achieves the same sort of relation to the stone as the government has to your pocketbook.

C

CYA: acronym:
(Cover Your Ass) Prime Directive for the starship Bureaucracy.

Cacophony: n.:
1) parliamentary debate. From *kaka,* traditional for the content, and *phone*, the sound-instrument that rules.
2) traditional elders' assessment of the music of youth.

Caduceus: n.:
a winged wand wrapped with snakes, traditionally the symbol of the medical profession, in recognition of the historical importance of snake oil to medicine.

Caffeine: n.:
legal cocaine.
Caffeine is still the most popular drug for relieving headaches, largely because such a high percentage of headaches are caused by caffeine withdrawal.
one of the chief raw materials used in the production of programming errors.

Cain: proper name:
one of a pair of traditional Christian icons of brotherly love.

Cajun: adj.:
pertaining to a cuisine and a culture which, like their French antecedents, are considerably spicier than those of their Anglo neighbors.

Calcium: n.:
miracle nostrum of the 80's.
The fad is so strong that calcium is touted as an additive to breakfast cereals, which are intended to by eaten covered with milk, the recommended primary source of the mineral.

Californicate: v.t.:
develop: cut all the trees, subdivide, pave and plant with houses that are "all made out of ticky-tacky and they all look just the same." [Malvina Reynolds]

Calumny: n.:
criticism, by an enemy.

Camera: n.:
the idol of the All-Seeing Eye, before which protestors perform and politicians posture. The primary agent of our Warholian 15 minutes of fame.

Campaign: v.i.:
place oneself on display for auction; advertise for buyers.

Campaign rhetoric: n.:
the candidates' attempt to ease the plight of the American farmer by supplying free fertilizer.

Can: n.:
bathroom; toilet.
   v.t.:
discharge unceremoniously.

Canape: n.:
personification of the *haut* dictum "don't eat with your mouth full."

Cancer: n.:
immortality, cell-by-cell, without let or hindrance.

Cannibal: n.:
food faddist who is convinced he has discovered a food that contains all the nutrients necessary for good health.
One who wants to be a man and believes the dictum "you are what you eat."

Can't: v.i.:
don't want to.

Capital: n.:
money. From the latin for head; so called because of the relationship between money and power: cf. "the golden rule"

Capital Punishment: n.:
the conservative's prescription for the disease of recidivism.

Capitol: n.:
from the latin *caput* (head); the seat of government. The destination of much of the capital in a politico-economic system: cf. "The buck stops here."
Where reporters would go to get their information "from the horse's mouth"; modern political practice has turned that all around.

Capitol Hill: proper name:
capital hill.

Capitol punishment: n.:
for individuals, it comes due on the 15th of April.

Capitol Steps: n.:
the venue where Caesar met his fate and the one where politicians have their true faces shown to their constituents.

Capracorn: n.:
soul food for Middle America.

Caput: adj.:
from the latin for head; dead, finished, destroyed. The usage may derive from observation of the Imperial Executioner or headsman. It may also derive from experience of the functioning of the Capitol, *q.v.*, or of capital, *q.v.*

Car: n.:
If a man's home is his castle, then the car is his fortress.

Carbon dioxide: n.:
Mother Nature's thermal blanket.

Carbon monoxide: n.:
dinosaurs' revenge.

Card-carrying: adj.:
not ashamed to admit affiliation, but not so insecure about it as to have to wear it on the sleeve.

Cardinal: n.:
senator of the Roman Catholic church; a priest and customarily celibate. Not to be confused with Roman Catholic senators, who are not customarily celibate, especially when from New England.

Caricature: n.:
1) a simplified representation, usually of a person, that emphasizes and exaggerates their most recognizable features.
2) an unflattering or insulting depiction.

Cart: n.:
fabulous horse precursor.

Carte blanche: n.:
sigil of the illiterate protester.

Case: n.:
1) the unit of professional activity of a lawyer, detective, policeman or doctor.

2) 24 bottles (12, if wine or hard liquor.)

Casino: n.:
modern temple to the twin icons of modern culture: Greed and Credulity; architectural monument to innumeracy.

Cassandra: proper name:
Greek prophetess who had the misfortune always to be correct, thereby eliminating her entertainment value.

Castrating woman: n.:
treble-maker.

Casus belli: n phrase:
"Why we fight."

Catastrophic health care: n.:
the kind where lawyers are involved, or where accountants make up the treatment rules.

Catamite: n.:
Greek for choir boy.

Catholic: adj.:
all-encompassing; universal. Named after the church in recognition of their view on the range of your behavior they should have control over.

Cato: proper name:
name of the Green Hornet's faithful Japanese (Filipino, after 1942) houseboy. Not to be confused with Kato...

Caucus: n.:
cabal.

Cause and Effect: n.:
a chance relationship susceptible to statistical analysis.

Caution: n.:
a defining difference between the truly adept professional and the fierily enthusiastic amateur. The symbols of caution are generally presented in yellow, in deference to the easily deflated ego of the amateur.

Cease fire: n.:
time appointed to hold your fire, unless a really good target appears; time out to reload.

Cedar: n.:
an tree that does in bugs faster than they can do it in.

Cedars of Lebanon: n.:
ancient species harvested to extinction to provide coffins for Beirut.

Celebrity: n.:
1) the fashionable side of notoriety; the imago of fame.
2) one who courts celebrity (1). Not to be confused with one who stalks…

Celibacy: n.:
safe sex, practiced by (ideal) priests, eunuchs, the right-wing version of teenagers, and old married couples.

Cellular phone: n.:
the reason that you can't get away from the office by getting out of the office.

Cenotaph: n.:
1) Judge Crater's crypt.
2) Campaign Reform Law.

Censor: n.:
an assassin who targets the mind, leaving the body free to toil. He does it with smoke, since, if he has a conscience, he can't go around looking into mirrors.

a patriot who believes in life, (limited) liberty and the flight from happiness. A few years ago, we could have said "(right-to-) life...", but censorship from the Left, once the bastion of free speech, has become rampant and even more insidious than the traditional blue-pencilling.

Censorship: n.:
the Comstock load: an attempt to throttle the mind and spirit of the public into as narrow a scope as those of the censor.

Censure: v.t.:
screen with fragrant, non-irritating smoke.

Certificate: n.:
a piece of paper widely sought in lieu of actual ability.

Chain reaction: n.:
a term used in physics to refer to an expansion that happens in the same way as the spread of gossip.

Champagne: n.:
Beverage of Champions. Arguably the best thing ever to come from the French Catholic church, though it must be said that Chartreuse has much to recommend it for that title.

Character: n.:
a rare attribute of politicians at the best of times, it has become a critical deficiency of Democrats, according to Republican campaign rhetoric.

Character assassination: n.:
the *lingua franca* of tabloid "journalism" and political campaigning.

Charge: v.t.:
1) invigorate a battery or an economy.
2) approach with the sort of careful consideration exhibited by bulls, elephants or basketball players.

3) prepare as bait for a lawyers' feeding frenzy.

Charisma: n.:
polite word for chutzpah in a political figure.

Charity: n.:
one of the triune muse of success: Faith provides the steadfastness to carry us through when times look bleak; Hope was the guiding light that led us first into the morass; Charity assuages our conscience for the things we had to do to win through.

Chartreuse: n.:
distillation of the essence of an alpine meadow at midsummer; arguably the greatest contribution of the Roman Catholic church toward the general benefit of civilization.

Chastity: n.:
a word that was upgraded from a lifestyle to a personal name in the Swinging Sixties.

Cheney: proper name:
the candidate with a thousand faces, this being seen as the ideal qualification for running for elected office.

Cherubic: adj.:
chubby.

Chic: adj.:
imitative of a different socioeconomic class or ethnos.
To be considered chic, the wealthy affect the denims and leathers of the lower classes and the weatherbeaten complexion of the outdoor worker; the proletariate wear imitations of the formal dress of the aristocracy; educated professionals buy CB radios so they can pretend to be ignorant truckers; college students get internet accounts so they can act like underdisciplined third graders—or trial attorneys—in public discussions.

Chicane: n.:
a twist or kink added to a race course to impede the normal flow of racing traffic and prevent the drivers from completing the race too soon, reducing the opportunity for commercials.

Chicanery: n.:
the practice of law.

Chilling effect: n.:
a hindrance to the side I support (or am beholden to); as contrasted with deterrence, which is a hindrance to the other side.

Chinatown: n.:
ethnic district in several major American cities; typically the location of Democratic National Committee headquarters.

Chocolate: n.:
in its Latin name, God-food. If sex is the favorite substitute for love, chocolate has become the favorite substitute for sex.

Cholesterol: n.:
a succubus for the Nineties.

Christ: proper name:
a prophet whose miraculous life among them managed to escape the notice of the most compulsive record keepers before the Third Reich.

Christian: n.:
one who follows the teachings of the New Testament so long as they are not too inconvenient or restrictive.
Literally, "anointed one," in honor of the status as a member of the Great Unwashed.

Christian Coalition: proper name:
a group seemingly dedicated to proving Justice Black's observation that "a union of government and religion tends to destroy government and to degrade religion."

Christian Science: n.:
   solipsism sanctified.

Christmas: n.:
   the day when we celebrate the birth of the Jewish Son of God with an orgy of buying and indebtedness. Conspiracy theorists note that the stores to which we indebt ourselves are disproportionately owned by Jews.

Church: n.:
   an institution for separating the poor from their goods by promising to repay after there is no further use for them.
   The observation that a man is accepted into a church for what he believes and turned out for what he knows is attributed to Twain.
   Fundamentalists will consider membership to be hellfire insurance.

Cigar: n.:
   fashionable mouth toy that, at its best, looks like a Cuban phallus and smells like a diaper pail.

Circle jerk: n.:
   member of the Inner Circle.

Circular reasoning: n.:
   logic designed to leave no loose ends.

Circumstances beyond our control: phrase:
   something happened we didn't plan on.

Civics: n.:
   the traditional name for the high-school course where they teach the fairy tale version of government.

Civil disobedience: n.:
   casual dress, cocktails and canapes after the rally; RSVP; don't do anything disgusting in front of the cameras.
   Note: we'll go home early if the cameras don't show up.

Civil rights: n.:
privileges properly reserved for the elite, which have been usurped by the Liberals to be squandered on everyone. A sort of a mild oxymoron, since very few of these rights were ever gained by the exercise of civility.

Civil servant: n.:
a functionary who typically delivers neither civility nor service.

Civil War: n.:
1) the cruelest oxymoron.
2) the historical event that created the country within a nation that is the South.
3) the recurrent theme of PBS pledge week.

Civilized: adj.:
decadent.

Class: n.:
1) glamor+panache: what all adolescents aspire to; as contrasted with the unit of school attendance, which adolescents abhor.
2) bounded social division.

   Mark Twain noted that America has no distinctly native criminal class except Congress.
3) a place where male and female students go, to sleep together with no hint of salacity.

Class system: n.:
fossilized social stratification. It has been observed that America has no class system, by which it is usually meant that America systematically has no class. This error of perception may be related to the observation that the bulk of the upper classes seem so utterly classless.

Classical: adj.:
in the tradition of the authors, artists or composers that you were required to study in school.

Classified: adj.:
potentially embarassing to the administration, or to any of the last thirty.

Classless society: n.:
one which derives its values from TV programming.

Clever: adj.:
knowing much, as contrasted with shrewd: knowing many.

Cloning: n.:
Man's high-tech way of promoting stagnation in the gene pool;
the supreme experimental test of the Nature vs. Nurture controversy.

Closed mind: n.:
one which obdurately refuses to be brought around to my way of thinking.
One which declines to be lured away from my way of thinking is not closed, merely perseverant.

Closet: n.:
locus of skeletons, gaiety or, if you're Fibber McGee, the contents of an average salvage yard.

Cock of the walk: n.:
a fellow who struts about as though he thinks he's a foot long.

Cockroach: n.:
a disgusting insect pest with a decided resemblance to certain members of my opponent's party.

Code: v.t.:
systematically change a message so as to make in illegible to anyone not a party to the method used. Common usages include references to "computer code" and "Code of Ethics."

Coerce: v.t.:
treat in the same manner as a government, its subjects.

Coffee: n.:
an addictive agent yielding the benefits of cocaine without the inconvenience of the narcotics squad.

Coiffure: n.:
$200 haircut.

Cola: n.:
a popular, mildly stimulating, slightly addictive soft drink.
acronym:
COLA: a popular, highly addictive additive to government entitlement programs.

Colin: proper name:
an organ of proper and useful, if distasteful, functionality, culminating in an asshole.

Colitis: n.:
a pain in the butt that extends throughout the belly.

Collectible: n.:
something collected or collectable; hence, something overpriced, faddish, usually either garish or banal, not very useful.

Collective: n.:
special name for a group of a type of entity, as a gaggle of geese, a flock of sheep, a conspiracy of lawyers…

College: n.:
an institution whereto parents send their children to learn things of academe that they can't learn in high school and the children go to learn things of life they daren't learn while living at home.

Color: n.:
an attribute of which you must be careful that it doesn't rub off on you, but which can't be washed off of you, no matter how diligent you are.

Color-blind: adj.:
unable to recognize more than one color.

Colored: adj.:

1) not black or white.

2) not black-and-white.

3) not white.
It all depends on where you ask.

Come and go: phrase:
agenda of the unfaithful spouse; actions of the unsatisying spouse.

Comfort: n.:
the lowest practicably maintainable level of pain.

Comfortably well off: adj phrase:
wealthy beyond the avarice of the common man, if not of the media star, pro sports player (or his agent) or stock trader.

Commerce: n.:
a modern institution evolved from the mutual exchange of meat and hides among hunters. The basis has remained unchanged: skin everything that moves. (with appreciation to David Astor)

Commercial: n.:
pothole in the Road to Entertainment.

Committed: adj.:

1) totally dedicated, as to a political or religious cause.

2) incarcerated, especially in an institution for the insane.

Committee: n.:
a group conjoined under rules of procedure for the purpose of legitimizing the prejudices of its most vociferous members.
Planning committees make plans, budgeting committees make budgets and morale among the men would be a lot higher if all the steering committees weren't headed up by women.
There are those who would hold that all committees strive to be steering committees, especially as regards their opponents.

Commodities trading: n.:
given that "commode" means "toilet", what do you think they're up to?

Commodore: n.:
undoubtedly, the rank of the Ty-D-Bowl man.

Common: adj.:
pertaining to one who is widely liked, but not by me.

Common enemy: n.:
the root of most friendships between nations and many between individuals.

Common ground: n.:
the bridge between seemingly disparate interests, as No-Mans'-Land to opposed armies, or the barroom floor to politicians and the journalists who report on them.

Common sense: n.:
a commodity notably absent from Government since their supply was used up to supply a title for Thomas Paine.
It has been observed that the most remarkable thing about common sense is that it's so uncommon.

Communicable disease: n.:
the variety that it's not polite to talk about.

Communication: n.:
the college course for jocks who can string three words together without saying "you know."

Communication satellite: n.:
celestial entity to which televangelists pray and offer sacrifice (of their followers' goods.)

Communicative disease: n.:
1) Talk Radio.

2) daytime talk show.

3) sermon.

Communal: adj.:
belonging to the community at large, which is to say, for the exclusive use of the most unscrupulous.

Communism: n.:
conservative Christianity with the principal names changed so that "God" becomes "State"; the "Bible", the "Manifesto"; "Moses", "Marx"; etc. Otherwise, they are barely distinguishable to the outsider.
Cold-War scapegoat for the failures of reactionary government and social policies in the West.
Standard-issue stalking horse for justifying expansion of police and government powers.

Community: n.:
a mythical affiliation based on a shared visible characteristic; e.g., black community, gay community, Jewish community, etc. A single shared characteristic, however blatant, is not enough to established shared interests.

Community service: n.:
to a liberal, a civic duty; to a conservative, a legal obligation.

Community standards: n.:
the published position of the most vocal conservative minority.

Commute: n.:
the morning ritual wherein we emulate the hamster with his little wheel.

Commuter airline: n.:
licensed gambling establishment.

Compact: adj.:
medium sized. As compact car, compact disc.

Compelling evidence: n.:
data presented on the point of a bayonet.

Compliment: n.:
a commodity of which it can truly be said that too much is never enough.

Composure: n.:
if you can keep your head while all around you are losing theirs, have you stopped to consider that you may be the cause?

Compromise: v.i.:
1) prepare the ground for future hostilities.
2) do it my way.

Compromised: adj.:
caught with his pants down (or her skirts up.)

Compulsion: n.:
an action which must be done, repetitively, in a certain way and which cannot be denied or resisted; characteristic of mental illness, religious observance, or soap-opera watching.

Computer: n.:
angel/devil of the latter twentieth century. A convenient scapegoat for clerical or human error.

Like fire, the computer is a useful servant and a dangerous master. The greatest failure of the computer as a servant is that it does precisely what we tell it to, not what we want it to.

The people who express the greatest fear of computers are those who never learned to type.

Con man: n.:
consultant with a bogus return address.

Conclusive: adj.:
supporting what I said all along.

Conditioned reflex: n.:
something learned so well as to happen without thought, like a conservative's getting red in the face on hearing the word "Communism" or the phrase "welfare mother." The product of intensive and extensive training.

Condominium: n.:
real estate scheme named for the condom: buy one if you want to get screwed.

Confidence builder: n.:
dishonest developer.

Confident: adj.:
misinformed.

Conflict: n.:
the offspring of Misunderstanding and of Understanding-only-too-well.

Conflict of interest: n.:
the difference between what the bank pays you to save money and what they charge you to borrow it back.

Conformity: n.:
the sacrifice we make to cultivate the approbation of those around us.

Confuse: v.t.:
present with more than one choice.
"I've made my decision; don't confuse me with facts."

Congress: n.:
1) a meeting for purposes of sexual intercourse.
2) an assembly for purposes of committing legislation.

Congressional hearing: n.:
a collective campaign appearance by the incumbents.

Congressional oversight: n.:
1) partisan hindsight;
2) the culture of pork.

Congressional Record: n.:
"A tale…full of sound and fury, signifying nothing." The "official version," a work of official fiction wherein your congressman may have his vote recorded the way he thinks you want to see it, rather than the way it was cast.

Conjugal: adj.:
pertaining to marriage.
Evaluated in the pair of popular expressions "conjugal bliss" and "ignorance is bliss."

Conjugate: n.:
reserved media name for the first scandal in Washington involving bigamy or other serious marital anomalies (adultery, being so widespread, does not qualify.)

Connoisseur: n.:
one guided by his tastes rather than his appetites.

Conscience: n.:
the "still, small voice" that intends to make sure you don't enjoy having a good time. It is most easily silenced by the application of

money, though it can be anesthetized with alcohol, or sometimes, dinner and a show or an evening out dancing.

When cited as the motivation for an action ("The senator voted his conscience"), it is usually just a euphemism for "pocketbook."

Conscientious: adj.:
either naive or hyperactive.

Consensus: n.:
the speaker's opinion, attributed to a group. This gives an air of authority and a chance to diffuse the blame.

Consequences: n.:
unplanned outcomes: when you drain the swamp, the alligators are certainly going to go somewhere.

Conservative: n.:

1) a former Liberal, who has since been mugged.

2) one who takes the dictum "man is born to trouble" as an instruction.

3) one who believes that that government is best that governs business least.

4) one who believes that the only proper use of tax dollars is the imposition of his religious views and mandated behaviors on those who do not share them.

Conservative court: n.:
one which dares to curtail the inalienable right of special interest groups to sue for having their feelings hurt.

Consistency: n.:
Doctrinairism.
A foolish consistency is the hobgoblin of little minds, adored by little statesmen and philosophers and divines. [Emerson]

Conspiracy: n.:
a group of people who agree with each other, but not with me.

Conspiracy theorist: n.:
one who belongs to a coterie who believe that the Government can't do anything well, except to maintain a huge, usually criminal, enterprise out of sight of the public—except, of course, for the theorist and his clique.

Constituency: n.:
body of contributors.
That element of the electorate represented by a sitting legislator.

Constituent: n.:
campaign contributor.

Constitution: n.:
the sole difference between a democracy and a mob. Our first and best defense against the tyranny of the majority.

Consultant: n.:
expert hired to come into a situation and tell you:

a) why you can't do what you want (or need) to do; or

b) why you don't need to correct the management practices that caused all the problems that you hired the consultant to correct; or

c) why you need to hire the consultant's firm to come in and retrain all your people and rework all your methods.

Consumer: n.:
the little, greed-fueled engine that drives the economy, to the cleaners.

Consumer advocacy: n.:
the nadir of public-service professions.

Consumption: n.:
a wasting and usually fatal disease, once of the lungs, now of the economy.

Contempt: n.:
a delicate emotion elicited by the contemplation of those of less value than ourselves; hence, contempt of court, contempt of Congress.

Contemptible: adj.:
admitted to the bar.

Contract: v.i.:
become smaller, especially with chilling.
   n.:
binding agreement to assassination or murder.
cf. "Contract with America."

"Contract With America": phrase:
contract on poor Americans.

Contraception: n.:
in the eyes of the right, an attempt to enjoy the entertainment without having to pay for the ticket.

Contradiction: n.:
the soul of spirited argument, if, and only if, you are a Monty Python fan.

Contrarian: n.:
a stock market player who goes against the mood of the market, i.e., one who buys when the news on the economy is good.

Contrite: adj.:
caught and trying to evade punishment.

Convenience: n.:
Euphemese for toilet.

Conventional: adj.:
  after the style of my parents or grandparents.

Conventional wisdom: n.:
  polite name for old wives' tales.

Conversation: n.:
  simultaneously the deepest foundation and highest pinnacle of civilization.

Conviction: n.:
  that property that distinguishes the professional politician from the amateur.

Cooperative: adj.:
  willing to do things my way.

Corpulent: adj.:
  advanced in one's progress toward becoming a corpse.

Corruption: n.:
  any lubrication of the wheels of government which does not result in the oiling of my pockets.

Cosa Nostra: proper name:
  Italian for "Our House", used as a term of affection for the House of Representatives, in recognition of their ongoing publicity and price-support campaigns.

Cosmetic surgery: n.:
  what some women require to remove their makeup.

Cost: n.:
  an economic property of an item or service that bears a relation to the price only in high-school civics courses.

Couch potato: n.:
  home-grown pseudo-vegetable. Herblock might characterize this as the TVegetable.

Counter terrorism: n.:
$3.00 a cup for coffee.

Counterfeit goods: n.:
plagiarism in the market place.

Counterfeiter: n.:
one who has applied private-sector initiative to the creation of financial resources.

Courage: n.:
a personal quality claimed by cowards and denied by heroes.

Courage of his convictions: n phrase:

1) confidence he will be sent to one of the white-collar prisons.

2) the belief that his fellow fanatics will declare him a martyr.

Court: n.:
an institution wherein laws are altered to suit the prejudices of the judge.
    v.t.:
attempt to seduce. Hence, the name of the place where lawyers practice.

Court house: n.:
the scene of many of the most egregious crimes in the community.

Court order: n.:
rubber stamp for police invasion; automatic indemnification of unfounded accusations.
Well applied, the first and finest defense against the depredations of tyrants, or the tyranny of the majority; well applied...

Courtesy: n.:
a medieval concept now out of favor, like slavery, manifest destiny, or the divine right of kings.
Unlike the others, it has not reappeared under a different name.

Couture: n.:
the business of conspicuous obsolescence.

Cow: n.:
the totem animal of Gary Larson.

Coward: n.:
a poltroon who turns away from dangers we claim we would have faced.

Cowardice: n.:
the best insurance against temptation. Frequently confused with self control, especially by those who lack the latter.

Coy: adj.:
shy by artifice, rather than by nature, reminiscent of the complexions of those who seek the label.

Coyness: n.:
the chief identifying characteristic of the unannounced candidate.

Coyote: n.:
the vaudevillain of the cartoon animal world; straight man to sheepdogs, rabbits and roadrunners.

Crap: n.:
the primary ingredient of life. The notorious optimist Theodore Sturgeon estimated the contribution as being 90%.

Crapulent: adj.:
drunk or hung over.
The origins of the term are related to the form-*ulent*, "full of". Compare: fraudulent, full of fraud; corpulent, full of body; it would appear to be a comment on the personality of the chronic heavy drinker.

Crash: n.:
1) the part of a car race the hockey fans come to see.

2) a drop in the Dow Jones of more than 5 per cent.

3) any unscheduled aircraft landing on a slow news day.

Creativity: n.:
the ability to find sufficiently obscure sources.

Credibility: n.:
a vestigial organ which incisive reportage has removed from the body politic.

Credit card: n.:
I'm sorry, but I can't top Bayan's "passport to the valley of the shadow of debt."
The modern method of indenture.

Credulity: n.:
the outstanding intellectual trait of the consumer, the voter or the devout.

Crimea: n.:
location of a river made famous by Julie London.

Criminal justice: n.:
1) the usual kind.

2) any judge who rules against my side.

Crisis: n.:
1) a problem which has caught the media's attention.

2) a situation which a politician needs to use as an excuse.

Crisis in Education: n.:
a failure in the school system exemplified in an inability to spell even common four-letter words, e.g. "lawyer", "Shiite."

Crisis management: n.:
the crucial ability to creat crises at need; the only form of production in which most managers exhibit any proficiency.

Critic: n.:
one whose inability to perform empowers his knowledge of how performance should be done.

Criticism: n.:
insightful evaluation of obvious deficiencies, if by me; wrongheaded attempts at character assassination, if of me.

Cross: adj.:
ill-tempered; angry.
    v.t.:
betray.
    n.:
burden, by implication unfair.
Symbol of the domineering Western religion.
"It's better to light one little cross than merely to curse the darkies"— Ku Klux Klan.

Cross dressing: n.:
wearing basketball shoes to do your aerobics.

Cross training: n.:
a form of athletic endeavor named for the disposition of its practitioners when they are interrupted.

Cross-functional: adj.:
disfunctional in more than one arena.

Cuba: *proper* n.:
Caribbean stalking horse for the American political system. The Miami Mafia hate it because the current government threw out theirs and spoiled their little party; the Republicans hate it because a) it's Communist (!) and b) it's poor, with no obvious resources for their corporate sponsors to exploit; the Democrats hate it because a) its human rights record is atrocious and b) they've never forgiven Castro for embarassing Kennedy at the Bay of Pigs.

Cul-de-sac: n.:
dead end street in an upscale neighborhood.

Culpability: n.:
the defining character of an incumbent.

Culprit: n.:
the accused one.

Cult: n.:
a religious sect younger than I am.

Culture: n.:
1) the forms and modes of art patronized by the moneyed and powerful.
2) the foul-smelling and frequently toxic collections of molds and germs that scientists grow on those little dishes of gelatin or that bachelors grow on their leftovers.

Curator: n.:
a professional collector who is not characterized by greed and secretiveness. Also, resident expert, display inventor, teacher *in absentia* and specialist librarian.

Curiosity: n.:
traditional felicide.

Curmudgeon: n.:
one who has stricken all artificial sweeteners from his literary diet.

Curriculum: n.:
the mold into which young minds are to be cast. Generally patterned on the neuroses of the loudest local pressure group.

Cursor: n.:
a common user interface named in honor of the reaction it routinely elicits.

Custom: n.:
> the self-enforcing law of the marketplace. Generally confused with morality or natural law by the obtuse.

Customer service: n.:
> a profession dedicated to the memory of Polly Adler.

Cute: adj.:
> able to elicit that instinctive inhibition which allows us to tolerate the young of the species.

Cyanide: n.:
> culinary staple of mystery writers everywhere.

Cybil: proper name:
> attendant to ovine domesticated cattle.

Cynic: n.:
> a vessel in whom the milk of human kindness has been curdled.

Cynicism: n.:
> an allergy to rose-colored glasses; a deficiency of the vision that allows one to see things as they are, rather than as they are portrayed in the press.

D

D'Amato: proper name:
New York pronunciation of tomato, a round, ruddy fruit known for its acidity and widely believed to be a vegetable.

Damocles: proper name:
famous Greek swordsman, early exponent of the high-tension overhead.

Dancing: n.:
the human adaptation of the mating display behaviors of other animals; commonly practiced by men as a prelude to mating and by women as a substitute for it.

Dangerous: adj.:
capable of causing damage. Frequently used in reference, inaccurately, to weapons or, hyperbolically, to men.

Dangerous drug: n.:
one I don't use; one my campaign contributors don't market.

DAR: acronym:
Drones, American, Reactionary.

Darwin: proper name:
to fundamentalists, an incarnation of the AntiChrist; favored scapegoat for the Right to account for their faulty appreciation of natural law.

Data: n.:
raw facts, before they have been kneaded into the form of information.

Data compression: n.:
the *Reader's Digest* principle, as applied by one's computer.

Date rape: n.:
revisionist crime of the 1980's and '90's; commonly a result of a young lady's having changed her mind in the cold, gray light of dawn.

Day care: n.:
an institution that allows parents to salve their consciences while pandering to their own greed.

DB Cooper: proper name:
American folk hero who disappeared from radar screens after a skyjacking; a criminal genius who demanded a parachute from the same people he was holding up for a million bucks.
The FBI composite drawing looks strikingly like Duke from the *Doonesbury* strip.

DC: n.:
1) polarized electrical charge flow, which tends uniformly away from the positive and toward the negative, always returning to its origin;
2) a polarized city on the eastern seaboard of the USA,...

Dead: adj.:
east of the Rockies, permanently registered to vote.

Dead right: adj.:
1) to leftists and civil libertarians, a consummation devoutly to be wished.
2) a frame of mind.

Deadhead: n.:
1) one who gets for free what the rest of us have to pay full rate for.
2) a nonproductive or unprofitable trip.
3) one on a perpetual deadhead (1 or 2) in a gaily decorated VW bus.

Dean: n.:
honorific assigned to people prominent in a field, on the theory that status confers wisdom.

Dear: adj.:
overly expensive; the traditional pet name of a spouse; the conventional salutation on a letter to your banker or lawyer.

Death: n.:
the goal toward which all life earnestly strives.

Death penalty: n.:
the effrontery of the state to demand of a convicted felon, after due process and many appeals and reviews, the same thing that it requires of its young men after drawing their numbers from a hat. The retribution which does not foster recidivism.

Death rate: n.:
a universal constant: one to a customer.

Debased: adj.:
[of money] adjusted toward its true value.

Debate: n.:
a media event where two (or more) candidates agree to share exposure in order to get free (usually prime) TV time to make campaign speeches. Debates are probably the only authentic cost-control

measure for major campaigns that has been implemented in modern history.

Debunk: v.t.:
throw out of bed.

Debut: v.t.:
show for the fourth time: leak, pre-release press conference, sneak preview, debut.

Decadent: adj.:
more refined or polished, or less abrasive, than I would choose to have them be.

Decapitate: v.t.:
abridge with extreme prejudice.

Decapitation: n.:
traditional way of informing a snake that it only has until sundown to live, or a king that he has overstayed his welcome, that his Divine Right has left.

Decency: n.:
prudery.

Deception: n.:
a trip down the garden path.
A classic deception was used during World War II to keep people from speculating on the purpose of the Oak Ridge plant: it was said that, owing to the shortage of horses to carry equipment into combat, the plant would be involved in constructing the forequarters of horses, which would then be sent to Washington, D.C., for the completion of the beasts.

Decision: n.:
act of desperation we are forced to when we run out of time.

Declassify: v.t.:
perform the bureaucratic equivalent of turning over a stone, in order to expose the secrets to the light of day.

Deconstruction: n.:
destruction; the intellectual equivalent of decomposition.

Decry: v.t.:
to rise in indignation against anything, especially after having been caught red-handed at it.

Dedication: n.:
sincerity, in deed as well as in word.

Deep in thought: adj phrase:
the way most peoples' minds work, about time to put on the hip boots, before it gets any deeper.

Defenestration: n.:
traditional extreme sport practiced by bullish stock brokers in celebration of a sudden bear market. Best observed as a spectator sport—from a respectful distance.

Deficit reduction: n.:
any moderation in the rate of increase of the burden we are piling on our childrens' shoulders.

Deficit spending: n.:
living on your childrens' and grandchildrens' earnings.
A doctrine to which the Republicans were late converts; they spent the '70s and '80s making up for lost time.
The whole concept can be viewed as an edited version of Swift's "Modest Proposal."

Definitely: adv.:
maybe.

Definition: n.:
what I want a word to mean.

Deist: n.:
one who believes in a god, but not in the God.

Delaney amendment: n.:
a law that should forbid the sale of vegetables as food, since they contain sunshine, a proven carcinogen.

Deliberate: v.i.:
sit in conclave for purposes of avoiding having to make a decision.

Delight: v.t.:
remove the bulb from.
  n.:
the sweetest, and stickiest, of the emotions, which we inherit from the Turks, along with the steam bath and the Thanksgiving fowl.

Delusion: n.:
a belief not in accordance with my own, especially when strongly held.

Demagogue: n.:
one who undertakes to inspire people in a cause that I disapprove of.

Democracy: n.:
a political system which, in the words of Shaw, "substitutes selection by the incompetent many for appointment by the corrupt few." Shaw had very limited experience of the American experiment with democracy.

Democrat: n.:
member of a political party symbolized by the jackass, an animal noted for its cooperativeness, the pleasantness of its disposition and the beauty of its speaking voice.

Demonology: n.:
a compendium of the names, titles and attributes of the senior members of the Legions of Darkness—sort of the medieval equivalent of the *Congressional Directory*.

Demonstrate: v.i.:
gather to mill about and chant mindless jingles in such a way as to get your picture on the TV; throw a group tantrum.

Deregulate: v.t.:
declare open season on consumers.

Deregulation: n.:
issuance of a blanket license to steal. When you look at the historical record of the famous successes of the days before "overregulation", it's no wonder they called them the Robber Barons.

Derivative: n.:
ticket in a high-stakes gambling game, where the broker plays against the brokerage as bank, using your money.

Descriptivist: n.:
one who believes that natural law is a principle to be discovered and used to predict the behavior of people or things. Typically a scientist or engineer.
Contrast prescriptivist.

Desirable: adj.:
rare, difficult of attainment, or forbidden.

Despair: n.:
the tender, nurturing emotion elicited by the inspection of IRS forms.

Destabilize: v.t.:
overthrow without admitting involvement in the act.

Destiny: n.:
the name we give to blaming God for our own carelessness.

Destructive: adj.:
the relation of the Congress to the Constitution.

Deterrent: adj.:
a quality of an institution or policy that, if successful, can never be proven effective, except by statistical analysis, which can be used to prove anything desired.

Deus ex machina: phrase:
religious broadcasting.

Developed nation: n.:
one in which there is more industrial than biological pollution.

Devil: n.:
one who must traditionally be paid when the pitch is not hot.

The Devil: proper name:
anthromorphized scapegoat for all the infirmities, inconsistencies and failings of humankind, especially those parts of it that belong to Western religions.
Hides in the details.

The Devil's Dictionary: book title:
the definitive dissertation on life and culture in turn-of-the-century America.

Devil worship: n.:
flash-in-the-pan media crisis wedding religious oppression with child abuse.

Devout: adj.:
having firm faith in the tenet that anyone offered a choice between one's chosen creed and its opposite will automatically choose the opposite. It automatically follows that the choice must never be allowed.

Dew: n.:
the footprints left by little cats' feet.

Diagnosis: n.:
the ascertainment of the source of an illness, generally reached by incantation, divination, or poking around in the entrails of the patient.

Diagonal: adj.:
slaunchwise, as the line in the prohibitionary circle.

Diagram: n.:
anorectic drawing.

Diamond: n.:
symbol of the ostentatious display of wealth, whether on a finger or in a stadium.

Diaphragm: n.:
a bumper designed to keep a man from knocking chips off his old block.

Diatribe: n.:
talk-show host's monologue.

Dice: n., pl.:
The plural of die, hence the usage of the term to refer to aerial combat and close auto racing.

Dictator: n.:
successful law-and-order candidate from a faction other than my own.

Dictatorship: n.:
a political system that has its trains running on time, but no one is free to travel on them.

Dictionary: n.:
a reference work useful to prove to yourself that you really did know how to spell that word. (Have you ever tried looking up a word you didn't know how to spell?)

Dictionaries are currently at the heart of a religious war between those who believe a dictionary tells you the meaning of what you said (the descriptivists) and those who believe it should tell you how to say what you want to mean (the prescriptivists.) The descriptivist dictionary is always out of date and therefore a barrier to clear understanding; the prescriptivist dictionary is an impediment to the evolution of the language and therefore a barrier to understanding anything that transpired after compilation of the dictionary.

Diet: v.i.:
impose upon ourselves in an attempt to look like what we are not: slim and athletic (and young.)
Diet-for-health is a modern fixation and is pursued primarily by the methods of old fashioned magic: [ethnic group] has some measure of health that I want, so I will imitate and exaggerate elements of their diet (preferably the distasteful ones—no pain, no gain) and it will give me the health I want.

Differ: v.i.:
(from me) err.

Difference: n.:
that which remains when all the similarities have been submerged.

Different: adj.:
wrong; dangerous; deserving of persecution.

Digital: adj.:
of or pertaining to the finger. Hence, when someone touts the "digital age," he is symbolically giving you the finger.

Digital communications: n.:
something men have been doing since long before there were computers.

Dildo: n.:
an appliance designed to fill a void in a woman's private life.

Dionysos: proper name:
Greek god of wine and the theater. Symbolically, the god of parties and good times; the patron of fraternities and sororities.

Diploma: n.:
a document which demonstrates that some school found the bearer certifiable.

Diplomacy: n.:
duplicity.
The apparent goal of diplomacy is to maintain a state of tension just short of outright warfare.

Diplomat: n.:
one who can invite you to go to Hell so smoothly that you actually look forward to the trip.

Disappoint: v.t.:
treat as an elected official does his constituents.

Disappointment: n.:
the fruits of hope.

Disaster: n.:
a predictable inconvenience that no one could be bothered to prepare for.

Disaster area: n.:
any area that Nature has made to look worse than the neighborhoods the Congress drive through (or around) on their way to the office.

Discourtesy: n.:
action that does not demonstrate prior deferral to my tastes.

Discover: v.t.:
invent. Especially as applied to evidence in support of the discoverer's preconceived notions.

Discriminating tastes: n.:
the judgement of someone who subscribes to the same magazines as I do, and has money.

Discrimination: n.:
the capacity for making distinctions based on subtle, frequently inconsequential, differences.

Discussion: n.:
a session where you can listen to my views.

Disenfranchised: adj.:
like a Democrat in the 104th Congress.

Disgrace: n.:
the condition toward which a political career naturally trends.

Disgust: n.:
the form of enthusiasm most often engendered by the realities of the political campaign or the demeanor of the campaigners.

Dishonor: n.:
a form of the afterlife, as defined in the phrase "Death before dishonor."

Disinformation: n.:
that which we tell, which would be a lie if you told it.

Disingenuous: adj.:
less than completely forthright, as when the Republicans chide a Democratic candidate for having overseen layoffs or taken a high salary.

Disk drive: n.:
a computer device designed to implement the loss of data.

Dismember: v.t.:
frighten, as "bibbity-bobbity-boo."

Disobedience: n.:
creativity in an underling.

Dispute: n.:
the detritus of Society, on which lawyers feed.

Disregard: v.i.:
attend with the same studious intensity that the Government exercises toward the rights guaranteed to citizens in the Constitution.

Dissemble: v.i.:
misrepresent, as the Prohibition movement claiming they were only for control and moderation—temperance. Given the historical record, perhaps we should encourage it more: temperance societies got their way for a while, but ultimately were discredited; firearm prohibition groups, dissembling as "control" activists, have been a nuisance but have done little actual harm; the absolutist Abolitionists precipitated the nastiest war in our history; the drug prohibitionists have founded and funded the greatest industry of crime and violence in all of history; the uncompromising anti-abortionists have been responsible for a reign of domestic terrorism unmatched by any admittedly political or religious movement.

Dissonance: n.:
harmony on acid.

Distress: n.:
discomfort commonly caused by observation of the good fortune of others.
   v.t.:
artificially age an artifact, so as to increase its value by making it seem to be an antique.

Dittohead: n.:
fellow traveller along the Disinformation Superhighway.

Diversity: n.:
opportunity for conflict and exploitation.

Divide and conquer: motto:
battle plan of those who believe "united we stand…"

Divination: n.:
reading the mind of God.

Divine Comedy: book title:
a made-for-tabloid-TV event costarring Hugh Grant.

DNA: n.:
the chemical of heredity; its helical shape is the reason genetics is so screwed up.

Doctor: n.:
one to whom the state has granted a license to kill.

Docu-drama: n.:
fiction based on an historical event, using the names of a couple of the original players and places.

Doggerel: n.:
to a literary critic, any poetry that rhymes and scans.

Dogma: n.:
an indulgence that futilely chases karma.

Dogmatic: adj.:
unwilling to be converted to my obviously superior position.

Doing the public's business: phrase:
doing the public, in a businesslike fashion.

Doldrums: n.:
a zone of inanity and tedium, devoid of excitement or events of interest. Pronounced "Dole-drums."

Dole: v.t.:
to administer parsimoniously; to hand out grudgingly.

Dole-othy: improper name:
one who's not in Kansas anymore. He hoped the Yellow Brick Road would be another name for Pennsylvania Avenue. It wasn't.

Domestic surveillance: n.:
the FBI plays KGB.

Donor card: n.:
a symbol that you'd like to be more useful in death than you were in life. If you can't take it with you, you may as well give it to someone who can use it.

Dope: n.:
one of a class of psychoactive substances, or a user of one of a class...

Double nickel: expletive:
an attempt to save fuel by making driving so unpleasant that people will choose not to travel. Legislation in the '70s based on an inadequate understanding of the technology of the '40s.

Doubletalk: n.:
talk delivered from both sides of the mouth.

Downsize: v.i.:
reduce the height of a pyramid by cutting off its base; assign your effectives as Mammon fodder.

Downsizing: n.:
economic massacre.

DP: *abbrev.*:
1) Displaced Person: a refugee.

2) Data Processing.
Hiring practices being what they are, a lot of data processing people are economic DPs.

Draft: n.:
[football, baseball, basketball, hockey] twentieth century legal slave market.

Dread: n.:
the gentle emotion engendered by the prospect of an upcoming political campaign and it attendant advertisements.

Dream: n.:
the carrot we use to lead ourselves through the doldrums of life.

Dream team: n.:
the other side's worst nightmare.

Drink: n.:
age-old lubricant of the human spirit. Having noted that as the drinker gets tight, his inhibitions loosen, the temperance movement decided on the necessity of prohibition.

Drive: v.t.:
operate an automobile. Observation indicates that the use of such verbs as control, pilot, maneuver is rarely warranted.

Drivel: n.:
the content of a campaign speech; or of advertising copy.

Drudge: n.:
one who toils meanly and monotonously, for hire.

Drug abuse: phrase:
use of any mood-altering substance that I don't use.

Drug free: adj phrase:
habituated to only those psychoactive, addictive substances which are marketed by corporate entities with large political constituencies.

Duck-bill: n.:
a dinosaur whose head was shaped like a baseball cap.

Duct tape: n.:
mankind's *homage* to gravity: that which holds everything else in the Universe together.

Due diligence: n.:
the level of precaution that my hindsight decides should have been necessary.

Dull: adj.:
insufficiently bright for me to see the reflection of myself.

Duly constituted authority: n.:
the side with the biggest battalions.

Dummy: adj.:
in computing, a meaningless variable used merely to hold a place until the place is needed; kind of the programming equivalent of a Vice President.

Dunce: n.:
a special scholar who is rewarded for his accomplishments by being allowed to sit in front of the class wearing the top part of a Klansman's hood.

Dust bunny: n.:
cultural icon which appears in honor of the season of spring cleaning.

Dusty: proper name:
the inevitable nickname for anyone whose last name is Rhodes.

Duty: n.:
a muzzle for conscience.
The stick we use to pursue our paths through the doldrums of life.

Dwarf: n.:
an unfortunate whose physical stature is comparable with the social stature of the average presidential candidate.

Dynasty: n.:
an institution designed to disprove the notion that ability is hereditary.

Dysphemism: n.:
opposite of euphemism; the language of the Right in describing the activities of the Left, or vice versa.

Dystopia: proper name:
proper name of worst of all possible worlds; the place where anything that can go wrong, does go wrong.

Dystopian: adj.:
of, or pertaining to: to the environmentalist, a Republican administration; to the developer, a Democratic administation; to the Libertarian, any administration.

E

Easter: n.:
> the day on which Christians celebrate the death of their god.
> Children see the juxtaposition of the death of the supreme authority with the conventional symbol of promiscuity—the rabbit—as a justification for sexual rebellion.
> Conspiracy theorists interested in the significance of the first Easter are referred to *The Passover Plot* by Schonfeld.

Ebonia: proper name:
> native land of American Inner City dwellers.

Ebonics: n.:
> a language subject to extensive miscommunication because of its overt resemblance to Moronics.

Ebullient: n.:
> acting as though they've had too much bubbly: unable either to shut up or to string together three sentences on the same topic.

Eclecticism: n.:
   a school of philosophy that treats the works of other schools as a Chinese menu: "I'll have this from column A, and these from column B, and a little of this moo shoo pork…"

Ecologist: n.:
   one who believes the world would be better off if only Noah and his family had been left at the docks.

Economist: n.:
   fictioneer who likes to work with budgets and ledgers, but whose arithmetic isn't good enough to qualify as an accountant.
   Someone who has misunderstood Kelvin. "When you can measure what you are speaking about, and express it in numbers, you know something about it" does not mean that the ability to make up numbers confers knowledge. Measurement means more than the assignment of arbitrary numbers chosen to advance a political philosophy.

Economy: n.:
   the china shop in which the bulls of Wall Street frolic.

Ecotopia: n.:
   mythical land where all industries are sustainable, all energy sources are renewable and the people live in harmony with Nature.

Edifice: n.:
   a complex building.

Editor: n.:
   traditional enemy of the writer.
   Editors are empowered to both the low justice and the high on the words entrusted to their care.

Editorial page: n.:
   the only part of the paper that admits to being slanted toward the publisher's prejudices. Not the only part of the paper that is so slanted.

Education: n.:
> the process of training the next generation to parrot the misconceptions and prejudices of the last.
> Those who can, do; those who can't, teach; those who can't teach write books about education.

Efficiency: n.:
> absence of compassion; antagonist to flexibility.

Effluenza: n.:
> disease brought about by pollution.

EFT: acronym:
> [Electronic Funds Transfer]
> 1) a way for your creditors or your PBS station to drain your bank account without any inconvenient pieces of paper, like bills, receipts, etc.
> 2) a way to move sums of money without having to handle valises full of $100 bills or have checks or other troublesome records lying around.
>
> n.:
> newt

Ego: n.:
> the commodity which demands the highest price for the least return.

Egoist: n.:
> one with such defective judgement as to think himself more important than me.

Egomaniac: n.:
> a boor who continues to talk about himself when he should be listening to me talking about myself.

Egotism: n.:
> the anodyne to the joint pains of incompetence and inadequacy.

Egotist: n.:
a headache brought on by severe I-strain.

Egress: n.:
the fabulously beautiful female egret, as featured in P.T.Barnum's museum.

Election: n.:
an event where we go to the polls to cast our vote for the candidate of our party bosses' choice.

Election fraud: n.:
how the other side wins.

Electra: proper name:
a young girl with a shocking love for her father.

Elephant: n.:
a mouse built on a cost-plus contract.

Elimination: n.:
Victorian euphemism for some of the biological Acts Which Must Not Be Discussed.
Nero Wolfe observed that "one of the deepest secrets of excellence [in art] is a discriminating elimination." Certainly, the NEA has taken his advice to heart.

Elitism: n.:
any system which presupposes the existence of a superior class that does not include me.

Elitist: n.:
one with the misguided notion that he and his friends are better than me or my friends.

Ellipsis: n.:
the "completion is left as an exercise for the reader" symbol; the author's tribute to the fact that you can stimulate your own imagination better than he can.

Email: n.:
modern anodyne for shyness.

Emasculated: adj.:
edited for television.

Embezzle: v.t.:
treat a financial trust in the private sector in the same manner as Congress treats the Social Security Trust funds in the public sector.

Embezzlement: n.:

1) private-sector pork barrelling; a crime wherein a businessman is caught acting as though he considered himself an electee.

2) the act of treating the corporate exchequer as though one were CEO, without having gained the title.

Emotion: n.:
the leavening that causes the bread of life to rise and become fragrant, light and delicious. What matters it, if for many of us the leavening is not yeast, but sourdough.

End of the world: n.:
what will surely happen if I don't get my way. Sometimes modified to the end of the world as we know it, if the matter isn't really earth-shattering.

Endorse: v.t.:

1) (in private life) accept responsibility for, as when you endorse a check.

2) (in public life) attempt to make something more attractive by renting out the value of the public recognition of a name or face, as when a celebrity endorses a product, or a public figure endorses a cause.

3) (political life) take a posture to appease a pressure group, without risking the consequences of actual support or action. Contrast with embrace.

Endorsements: n. plural:

the endorphins of the body politic: they are the reward for running, they reduce sensitivity to outside stimuli, and they impair the ability to react smoothly, quickly or strongly.

Energy: n.:
the ephemeral face of matter; the persistent face is inertia.

Enemy: n.:
ex friend.
Always choose your enemies carefully, for they are the people you end up most like.

The enemy of my enemy is my friend: motto:
a bit of fallacious philosophy that has been responsible for entirely too much of American foreign policy.

Enjoyable: adj.:
sinful.

Ennui: n.:
the goad which impels the wealthy in the same way as hunger, the poor;
the greens from which our salad days were cut.

Entitlement: n.:
everybody wants a slice of the pie; nobody wants to have to fork over the dough. Americans have the idea that if you can afford (or get away with) something once when times are good, it should be guaranteed forever.

Entropy: n.:
the degree of disorder in a system, which constantly increases—a common property in physics and politics. Entropy and the cost of living are the only things in nature that consistently run uphill.

Environment: n.:
the resource we consume in disposing of our wastes, as we use up paper towels in cleaning up spills.

Environmentalist: adj.:
pertaining to a group of activists who seem to believe that if they don't let us put it anywhere, radioactive waste will go away, that the one cancer caused by use of an agricultural chemical is worse than the ten cancers and three starvations it prevents, that timber companies should be forced to turn their lumber back into trees and plant them in the forests,...

Envy: n.:
the consequence of observing another's good fortune.

Epidemiology: n.:
Medical Statistics.
This is the science that enables us to prove that cigarettes cause cancer, or eating rice causes yellow skin.

Equal: adj.:
favored.

Equal Opportunity: n.:
privileged status—"and the sins of the father shall be visited on the sons."
Activists and Liberals routinely confuse equal opportunity with equal outcome. Policies based on this confusion constitute much of the barrier to achievement of a genuinely egalitarian culture.

Equivocate: v.i.:
speak in the forthright and uncompromising manner of a candidate during an election campaign.

Err: v.i.:
to hold views not in consonance with mine.

Erstwhile: adv.:
once upon a time.

Eructation: n.:
popular participatory sport of adolescent males. Vocalization with the intellectual content of a campaign promise.

Erudite: adj.:
possessing the kind of knowledge that comes from lots of reading and lectures, but no actual experience.

Eschew obfuscation: motto:
Erudite formulation of "keep it simple, stupid."

Et cetera: phrase:
the linguistic equivalent of the hand-waving a magician does to distract attention from the trick.

Eternity: n.:
the only period of time longer than the presidential campaigns. The next shorter period is the NBA playoffs.

Ethnic: adj.:
having religion or ancestry different from mine.

Ethnic slur: n.:
the tool we use to sever our bonds to the humanity of our foes. Killing people is murder; killing gooks, slopes, ragheads, kikes, the list goes on and on, is pest control.

Ethnocentric: adj.:
believing that the quirks and foibles of one's family and friends are laws of the universe.

Etiology: n.:
the study of the development of the manifestations of a physical illness; not to be confused with the homonymous ideology: the manifestation of mental or emotional illness.

Etiquette: n.:
a compendium of rules of behavior which, if followed carefully, will allow you to avoid being impolite. It is the custom to impose rules of etiquette rather than to teach courtesy, which would encourage being polite.

Etymology: n.:
the study of the derivation and variations of words. Sometimes confused with entomology, the study of the history and variations of bugs. The two converge in the field of computer programming, the art of developing and implementing bugs in computer languages.

Eulogy: n.:
a speech inventing the merits of the departed.

Eunuch: n.:
a man who has been treated with the same care and consideration we ordinarily lavish on our pets.
The traditional eunuch runs to the same physique as the standard couch potato.
The stereotype eunuch is pudgy, fussy and non-aggressive, with greatly reduced appetites, except, perhaps, for food, making him nearly the ideal man in the eyes of many Western urban women. Like most stereotypes dealing with sexuality, this one is not very accurate.

Euphemism: n.:
the language spoken by newscasters, admen or lawyers for the defense.

Europe: n.:
a geographic region named for a Greek lady who was raped by a bull claiming to be invested of a God, thereby setting the pattern for her namesake's political and social history.

Euthanasia: n.:
the execrable act of effectively alleviating terminal suffering.

Evangelism: n.:
putting the principle "misery loves company" into practice.

"Everybody does it": mantra:
"I did it, and I got caught."

Evil: adj.:
distasteful or inconvenient to me; such that I would feel ashamed if caught at it.

Evil Empire: n.:
one in competition with mine.

Evolution: n.:
progressive change without violence, except by those who deny the reality of the change.

Exactly: adj.:
approximately.

Exaggerate: v.t.:
1) prepare for inclusion in a news report or a political speech.
2) discuss the merits of the dead.

Excessive force: n.:
force used against my side.

Excise: v.t.:
   to remove bodily and/or totally.
      n.:
   a tax or license, designed to excise one's income.

Excrement: n.:
   the substance of my opponent's platform.

Excuse: n.:
   the lonely sentinel who wards between us and our unwanted obligations.

Executive: n.:
   one whose duty is to act as executioner of the organization's plans and goals; and, especially, workforce.

Executive privilege: n.:
   a cloak for the President to use when wrapping himself in the flag no longer offers enough protection.

Exercise: n.:
   self-torture undertaken in an effort to polish the soul without having to give up the activities and attitudes that tarnished it in the first place.

Exon: n.:
   in a gene, the part that promulgates useful information;
   not so in the Congress.

Expanded consciousness: n.:
   swelled head.

Expectation: n.:
   preparation for disappointment.

Experience: n.:
   the one thing of value we bring home from our most humiliating defeats. Experience makes the difference between a preacher and a teacher.

Expert: n.:
1) one who has got enough of his writings published that people think he knows what he's talking about.
2) twentieth-century replacement for the Oracle at Delphi.
3) has-been, high-pressure drip.
   adj.:
having enough certificates and credentials to overawe doubters.

Expert opinion: n.:
one which agrees with, or supports, my own.

Explain: v.t.:
confuse.

expletive: n.:
a word pronounced explosively to relieve emotional stress; generally deleted from transcripts and bleeped from TV shows.

Exploit: v.t.:
use in any way I do not approve of or profit from.

Extol: v.t.:
invent; as to extol the virtues of the honored guest.

Extort: v.t.:
apply the methods of the IRS in the private sector.

Extravagant: adj.:
more generous with a limited resource than I would be, or claim to be; especially if it's my resource.

Extreme: adj.:
mindless, as extreme skiing, extreme magic, extreme political positions.

Extreme sports: n.:
activities undertaken in pursuit of a Darwin award, offering the added incentive that, in most cases, both the participant and the society he is flouting will be winners.

F

Fable: n.:
a fictional anecdote intended to sugar-coat an ideological message—rather like a report by a Presidential Commission.

Face: n.:
standard currency of Asian savings accounts; of greater value than gold or life.

Face your fears: motto:
look into a non-rose-colored mirror.

Fact: n.:
1) what I believe.
2) what I want you to believe.

Factoid: n.:
a trivium which, while showing the appearance of a fact, usually ensconces an urban legend or a minor element of propaganda.

Fad: n.:
what occupies the public attention in lieu of interest or enthusiasm; populist fashion.

Fair: adj.:
   1) the way I want it to be; favorable to me.
   2) a) equitable
      b) less than good.

Fair-haired boy: n.:
   larval form of Great White Hope.

Fair share: n.:
   of taxes: from me, none; from business, their share, plus enough to make up for my share.
   of benefits: for him, none; for me, all I can carry off.

Fair trial: n.:
   one which has the outcome I desire: for the plaintiff, conviction, for the defendant, acquittal.

Fairy: n.:
   one of the class that make most of the magic happen for Hollywood and Broadway.

Fairy tale: n.:
   a story that begins "Once upon a time…" or that has a Washington DC dateline.

Faith: n.:
   religion's substitute for reason.

Fallacy: n.:
   what you believe, but I don't.

Familiarity: n.:
   contemptuous breeder.

Family-: adj. prefix:
   insipid.

Family-oriented: adj.:
   sanitized to the point of having lost all savor.

Family leave: n.:
a tax-in-kind on not having children. Co-workers of people who want to stay away from work to take care of children have to absorb the workload of the stay-away.

Family values: n.:
a package of policies designed to guarantee a continuing source of income for those churches that perform marriages.

Fan: n.:
adulator; if the team has a chance at the title, idolator.

Fanatical: adj.:
possessing a degree of commitment or devotion, to a cause I deplore, which is greater than any I can muster for those I endorse.

Fantastic: adj.:
signature euphemism of better charm schools everywhere.

Fantasy: n.:
spice for the intellect.

Fashion: n.:
a body of style chosen to create an effect:
the rich affect expensive fashions to intimidate their inferiors and distinguish themselves from the masses;
the middle classes imitate earlier fashions of the rich to try to look prosperous and important;
the young affect fashions to offend and irritate the previous generations.

Fat: adj.:
weighing more than me.

Fat of the land: n.:
traditionally inexhaustible source of wealth. Modern inexhaustible source of wealth for faddists in diet, exercise, pills and liposuction.

Fault: n.:

1) a character trait other people have.

2) something we admit to freely, when caught red-handed.

Faultless: adj.:

blessed with selective memory.

Fax: n.:

short form of facsimile: imitation. To send a fax is to make an imitation communication.

FDA: acronym:

Fuddy-Duddy Association. Another regulatory agency that makes "scientific" decisions based on the pressures exerted by lawyers.

Fear: n.:

the great motivator of emotions.

Feast: v.i.:

overeat.

Federal Reserve Chairman: n.:

high priest in the temple of Mammon.

Feeding frenzy: n.:

a phenomenon in the behavior of sharks and a few other cold blooded carnivores which bears a startling resemblance to the media's response to a spectacular story.

Feelings: n.:

how we steer our lives when it would be too much trouble to think.

Feeping creaturism: n.:

an element of Marketing, which is used to justify the adage: "There comes a time in the life of every project when it becomes necessary to shoot the engineer and go into production."

Female: adj.:

oppressed, victimized, incapable of violence, innocent.

Femi-Nazi: n.:
conservative personification of their jealousy at someone's having adopted their policy of intolerance.

Feminism: n.:
according to their bumper sticker, "the radical notion that women are people." This omits the fact that the movement also includes the equally radical notion that men aren't.

Feminist: n.:
one who, on hearing the Lerner and Loew song "Why can't a woman be more like a man?" immediately thinks of changing men to meet the requirement.

"*Fiat lux:*" phrase:
Latin for "Big Bang."

Fiat money: n.:
money backed by the full faith and credit of the issuing government; money without real value.

Fib: n.:
apprentice fabrication.

Fiber: n.:
nutritional lodestone of the Abstemious.

Fiber optics: n.:
in spite of the misleading name, this is not vision enhancement for that set who use Preparation H in place of Brylcreem.

Fiction: n.:
principal content of the news media; the core constituent of modern reportage.

Fifth Amendment: n.:
a constitutional protection made notorious by being heavily used by organized crime figures, Communists, subversives, members of the National Security Council, and aides to the President.

Figurehead: n.:
one who leads in the same way as the statue at the prow steers the ship.

"Figures don't lie": clause:
arrant—and errant—propaganda from the accountants, who believe it, and the statisticians, who put the lie to it every time they publish. Poll takers rely on the public's having been brainwashed into accepting it.

On an unrelated, but more pertinent, note, anyone who believes that figures don't lie lacks understanding of the traditional phrase "Body by Firestone." And they've certainly never watched the remarkable Miss Carol Doda in action.

Filibuster: n.:
flatus of the body politic.

Filicide: n.:
instinctive impulse of the middle-aged male when confronted with the adolescent male. The entire success of the species hinges on the cultural inhibition of this reaction.

"Finder's keepers": adage:
1) it's not something I lost, or

2) it's something I found.

Finesse: n.:
an element of which advertising and political speeches are notably deficient.

Finger: n.:
the fundamental agent of digital communications.

Fiscal: adj.:
off-schedule; as fiscal year, fiscal responsibility.

Fiscal year: n.:
a generous artifice of industry by which they free up accountants for consumers to use during the April 15 crush.

Fish: n.:
Nature's forethoughtful means for filtering mercury, DDT, and other pollutants from our natural waters.

Fisherman: n.:
a person who is not a person in the eyes of the "owls or people" people in the Spotted Owl controversy.

Fist: n.:
the "open hand" of Government.

Fit: adj.:
fortunate.

n.:
a politician's or preacher's standard reaction to any proposal that would increase personal autonomy.

v.t.:
force into an undersized container, as "I can still fit [myself] into the clothes I wore in high school."

Fix: v.t.:
1) (of an object) render incapable of movement or roving.
2) (of an entity) remove the impetus toward roving.

Flag: n.:
1) standard printed on overly combustible material.

> In their attempt to assign iconic status to the flag, the right attempted to pass a Constitutional amendment banning the burning of flags. One commentator noted that such a position would be supportable if an exception were made for flags

wrapped around a politician, in which case the burning should be compulsory.

2) winding sheet for the career of many a demagogue self-styled as patriot.

Flag desecration amendment: n.:
a right-wing movement that seeks to overturn both the First Amendment and the first Commandment.

Flash in the pan: n.:
a showy start with no followthrough, much like a campaign promise.

Flasher: n.:
a dim bulb who puts himself out in a vain attempt to brighten up his deficient little life.

Flat tax: n.:
an assessment that leaves you flat broke.

Flattery: n.:
the food of fools; the insincerest form of imitation.

Flatus: n.:
an emission from the lower end of the alimentary canal, the physical properties of which are startlingly similar to the intellectual properties of most emissions from the other end of the alimentary canal.

Fleece: v.t.:
to relieve the sheep of their burden of hot, itchy wool.
The primary reason that a shepherd maintains a flock.

Flint: n.:
the material of which conservative hearts are fashioned. The advantage of this construction is the protection against bleeding at the slightest provocation.

Flirtation: n.:
fraternization with the enemy in the War Between the Sexes.

The establishment of sexual tension without the necessity of sexual intention.

Flock: n.:
1) aggregation of sheep.
2) congregation of churchgoers.
"If the good Lord hadn't meant for me to shear them, He wouldn't have made them sheep."

Flower child: n.:
counter-culture dropout of the '60s. So named for their dedication to the aroma of fertilizer.

Fog: n.:
air having the clarity of a Congressional speech.
Caused by the cooling of hot air, fogs dissipate when exposed to the light of day.

Foley: n.:
a catheter: a device to tap the contents of the body, designed so that the owner of the body can't control the draining.

Folk: adj.:
polite form of "masses".

Folk wisdom: n.:
an element of popular mythology, alongside "common sense" which presumes that superstition is a basis for ordering ones life.
A social order which teaches, simultaneously, "absence makes the heart grow fonder" and "out of sight=out of mind."
Ideally, the Wisdom of the Ages; much more often, the "wisdom" of the aged.

Folly: n.:
a bit of bad judgement that I wouldn't have made.

Food: n.:
the proper function of Man, from the worm's point of view.

Fool: n.:
1) human.
2) the most important of a king's advisors, being the only one free to speak his mind without (much) fear of consequences. The relationship of freedom from consequence and foolishness has been inverted and endured into the modern Cabinet.

Foolhardy: n.:
courageous in support of a cause I don't believe in.

Foolish: adj.:
lacking the my fine, discriminating judgement; fatuous; credulous; enamored of the other side.

Football: n.:
in America, a violent sport offering vicarious release; in the rest of the world, a vicarious sport offering violent release.

Forbes: proper name:
an alphabetic location between forbear and forbid seems to have foreshadowed the electorate's reaction to a would-be candidate.

Forbid: v.t.:
make attractive to youths and fools.

Foreign Affairs: n.:
why congressmen take overseas junkets.

Forgive: v.t.:
give up on. But never forget.

Formal: adj.:
artificially structured; ritualized; divorced from practical, everyday life. As formal education.

Formality: n.:
pointless gesture; frequently performed for the benefit of the press.

Fornication: n.:
unlicensed license.

Forswear: v.i.:
converse on the links.

Fortunes of war: n.:
military contractors' profits; profiteers' bank accounts.

Founding fathers: n.:
a group of seditious and traitorous men involved in a sworn undertaking to overthrow their established government.

Fountain of Youth: n.:
an American Holy Grail, sought after in health clubs, plastic surgery practices, herbalists' shops, Swiss goat-gland clinics. The quest goes on, because anyone who doesn't believe in the fountain of youth hasn't changed many diapers.

Fox: n.:
the feminine of wolf.

Fraternize: v.i.:
sell out cheaply.

Fratricide: n.:
the final expression of brotherly love, as it is usually practiced; the longest-standing documented practice of Christianity.

Free and democratic election: n phrase:
free, because there is no cover charge at the polls; democratic, because, in the Tammany and Chicago traditions, everyone gets to vote for the candidate his alderman supports.

Free enterprise system: n.:
absence of restraint on the rapacity of businessmen.

Free Market: n.:
one without an admission charge other than the requisite bribes to appropriate government officials.

Free speech: n.:
speech paid for, or in a forum paid for, by someone else.
Free speech is the coin of the marketplace of ideas; like other coinages, it is routinely debased by the intervention of Government.

Free trade: n.:
commerce unencumbered by the attentions of officials not friendly to my activities.

Free Willy: n phrase:
bane of the gigolo.

Freedom: n.:
another word for nothing left to lose.

Freedom Fighter: n.:
a terrorist working against my enemy.

Freedom of expression: n phrase:
a supposed entitlement to interfere with the lives of others and to destroy their property in protest of a system which has made me wealthy beyond the dreams of previous generations (but not of mine.)

Freedom of Speech: n phrase:
a right which may be exercised openly, except when it may offend the neuroses of anyone represented by a politically connected pressure group.

Freeman: n.:
slave of a different master than mine.

Freshen: v.t.:
dairyman's euphemism for impregnate. If your host offers to freshen your drink, keep an eye on him.

Freud: proper name:
 a student of the mind whose personality theories authentically depicted the obsession with sex that permeated his society; progenitor of the profession of psychiatry, hence the frequent misspelling of his name as "Fraud."

Friendship: n.:
 the adamantine basis of all social commerce. In men it will stand any strain except a small loan, in women, except criticism of her children, although differences in taste in decorating will put a strain on it.

Frigid: adj.:
 of a woman, not inclined to respond to my style of lovemaking.

Fringe: adj.:
 away from the center; at or near the limits.
 We tend to forget that the description applies equally to the leading edge and the trailing.

Frontier: n.:
 an old institution, renewed in 1960, wherein there is more room for one's elbows. The final version has little except room.

Frontrunner: n.:
 the candidate with the most knives in his back.
 The frontrunner must always keep in mind Satchel Paige's dictum: "don't look back—somebody might be gaining on you."

Frustration: n.:
 the emotional state resulting from a comparison of the candidates, stemming from the realization that yet again we are faced with the evil of the two lessers.

Fugitive from justice: n.:
 sitting legislator.

Fun: n.:
 a pasttime to which fundamentalists seem fundamentally opposed.

Fundamental: adj.:
a term derived from fund—pertaining to money—and mental—pertaining to the mind or thought—refering to someone who thinks with his pocketbook, or with that portion of the anatomy adjacent to where the pocketbook is worn.

Fundamentalism: n.:
orthodoxy in a religion I don't agree with.

Fundamentalist: n.:
one who espouses the literal accuracy of his personal mythology. From "fundament", that portion of the anatomy used to polish chairs, wherein resides the intellect.

Funny: adj.:
whatever makes you laugh. Funny is in the eye of the beholder, but a pratfall is always funny, in any time or clime, if only to the beholder.

Fuzzy: adj.:
inaccurately perceived; out of focus; especially in "warm fuzzies."

Fuzzy logic: n.:
logic which processes imprecisely formulated inputs to produce inadequately defined conclusions.
Warm-fuzzy logic is another form of rationalization.

G

GAAP: acronym:
generally footnoted in annual reports as "Generally Accepted Accounting Principles."
This is of course inaccurate, as it is widely known that accountants have no principles. More nearly properly rendered as "Generally Accepted Accounting Practices."

GDP: acronym:
new name for GNP; Heaven for the GOP.

GOP: *initials*:
Grand Old Party: the Republican party. Generation Of Patriots to their defenders, Greedy Old Plutocrats to their detractors.

GRAS: acronym:
Generally Regarded As Safe; the FDA's version of "if it was good enough for Grandma it's good enough for you."

Gadfly: n.:
a source of irritation that provides no value to anyone but the gadfly; cf. consumer advocate, tax activist.

Gaffe: n.:
a declaration in the idiom of the public figure.

Gag: n.:
a certain class of jokes; so named for the reaction they elicit.

Gag rule: n.:
a judge's order to shut up the lawyers outside the court room; so called because they are such a bad joke.

Galilee: proper name:
traditional Land of the Risen Son.

Galley: adj.:
a term that has two common occurences in English: galley slave and galley proof. Writers and editors are aware of the reasons for the association.

Gang: n.:
surrogate family for the child who needs a whole village to raise him.

Gang-banger: n.:
gangster wannabe. The basic banger is a lad who tries to look like a man by wearing clothes that make him look like an 8-year old wearing his dad's old clothes.

Gavel: n.:
miniature mallet. Used by a sitting judge to make symbolic striking motions in exercising control of the court. This is often a sublimation of his desire to bash in the head of one of the attorneys.
The miniaturization of the gavel, relative to its ancestral mace, illustrates the diminution of the judge's authority. The tendency of judges to overstep their authority represents an attempt to reverse this historical decline in power.

Gay Nineties: n.:
> the last decade of the 19th century. Activists had hoped to reprise in the 20th, but the accession of the religious right makes the characterization of that decade as the Anti-gay 90's much more realistic.

General anesthesia: n.:
> a medical procedure which has a similar effect on attention, awareness and sensitivity to the experience of falling in love.

General confusion: n.:
> senior staff officer.

Genetic engineering: n.:
> 1) technology from someone born to the craft.
>
> 2) heir-conditioning.
> Genetic engineering is a pastime of humans since the first canine decided to wander into a *Homo* encampment. It is the wonder of the ages, which has empowered us to feed the Hungry and clothe the Poor. Now, when the prospect for reducing the numbers of trials and errors is at hand, it has been declared Evil.

Genial: adj.:
> possessing a character trait—cheerfulness—seldom found in genius.

Genital: adj.:
> sexual; from the latin for "beget." The same root gives us "genitive": possessive.

Genius: n.:
> cleverness, or a person exhibiting that cleverness, especially if I wouldn't have thought of it myself but could recognize it quickly when I saw it.
> Edison's formula of 99 percent perspiration and 1 percent inspiration misleads many to the conclusion that if they waste enough energy working up a sweat, people will think they're smart.

Genocide: n.:

1) a legitimately dirty word that has been debased to mean any attempt to move an ethnic pressure group back toward merely equal rights.

2) activist term for birth control.

Gentile: n.:
one who lacks gentility.

Gentleman: n.:
one who acts in such manner as never to give offense—unintentionally; a man who recognizes and honors the responsibilities of elevated status, in addition to its perquisites. This class of behavior is so much a luxury that it was once restricted to the landed classes; now it seems to be restricted to fictional characters.

Geocentric universe model: n.:
egocentric universe model.

Geography: n.:
that discipline which allows us to document that we are lost.

Gerbil: n.:
a rat with a really good press agent.

Gerontocracy: n.:
the result of the advantage of incumbency; the ultimate goal of the Gray Panthers and of southern-state districting practices.

Gerontology: n.:
a branch of gastroenterology: the study of old farts.

Gestalt: adj.:
of a philosophic principle which holds that the whole is greater than the sum of the parts.
This result is generally achieved by the straightforward procedure of not counting all the parts.

"Get government off the backs of the people": *slogan*:
get the police out of the boardroom and back into the bedroom.

Get off: phrase:
get it on, successfully.

Gigolo: n.:
a man who has enough faith in his opinion of himself as a great lover to stake his livelihood on it.

Gin: n.:
Satan's sweat, to the temperant; Tears of the Lamb to the tippler.

Gingrinch: n.:
portmanteau word containing gin, a seducer of wills, and *grinch* (q.v.), a notorious killjoy; hence, the personification of a hangover.

Glamor: n.:
marketable substitute for beauty.

Gland: n.:
popular scapegoat for obesity.
"Your glands are fine. You are suffering from an overactive fork."

Glans: n.:
part of a sex organ: "You and your glans | make this romance | too hot to handle."

Glass: n.:
architectural material used for the construction of ceilings in companies that hire women.

Glory: n.:
traditionally, one of the two great motivators, the other being love. They missed fear, and never underestimate the power of human spite.

God: n.:
the entity created by the religious to stand as scapegoat for their greed and lack of foresight.

Godzilla: proper name:
mascot of Japan, Inc.

Golden Age: n.:
the "Good Old Days;" fictitious product of a deficient memory; the result of looking back through rose-colored glasses.

Golden arches: n.:
proof that he is smart enough to piss in his boots.

Golden fleece: n.:
1) tax credits for political contributions.

2) hair transplants paid for with tax dollars.

The Golden Rule: credo:
Do unto others.
The fundamental social principle of Christians—and most others.
phrase:
whoever has the gold gets to make the rules.
   n.:
the civil code for living under the Law of Moses.

Golf: v.i.:
chase a little ball along grassy fields saturated with pesticides, in the direct sun, raising one's stress level; all in the name of health.

Good: adj.:
I like it.

Good Cause: n.:
one I approve of.
The question is, why do good causes generally produce such bad effects?

Good taste: n.:
esthetic judgement that coincides with mine.

Goose: n.:
important bird of folklore, noted for its melodious voice, its incisive cleverness, its aggressiveness and its monogamous mating habits

Gore: n.:
1) lap piece of a lady's garment.
2) the gruesome inner contents of the body.
3) one section of the skin of a hot-air balloon.
   v.t.:
1) something we do to other peoples' oxen to get them to change their perspective.
2) to bore with great force.

Gossamer: n.:
fabric as substantial as a politician's assurances, as tranparent as his protestations.

Gossip: n.:
the most sought-after currency in social commerce. If you can't say anything nice about someone, pass along the most recent gossip.

Government: n.:
the agency that spends what you earn; a monument to the proposition "What's yours is mine, what's mine is my own."

Graffiti: n.:
1) proof of the illiteracy of a race which has learned to write on walls.
2) publishing by the inconsiderate for the illiterate.
3) "Mene, mene, tekel upharsin."

Graft: n.:
the lubricant of the machinery of public policy.

An institution which allows an official to spend millions in pursuit of a hundred thousand dollar per year job, profitably.

There is a subtle, but important, difference between graft and baksheesh, with which it is often confused: baksheesh is payment for an official's doing his job, graft is payment for his evading his job.

Gram: n.:
metric measure for the weight of something of not much substance, except for drugs. Extensively used for weighing with balances, especially for commodities of high price.

Gramm: n.:
political measure of not much substance. Extensively out of balance toward the high-priced side.

Grandparent: n.:
a parent empowered to take revenge on its children.

Gratitude: n.:
resentment in party clothes.

Gravity: n.:
that property of Nature that causes things to fall down instead of up. The only energy source that has never been known to fail.

Great White Hope: n.:
a shark that entertains the troops at Christmas.

Great: adj.:
large;
good.
which is, to the modern American psyche, two ways of saying the same thing.

Greater good: n.:
a legal defense wherein the defendant undertakes to convince the court that the defendant's beliefs and values should be honored above the law. Commonly used by environmental activists who have

committed sabotage and by Right-to-Life advocates who have committed arson or murder.

Greatest tax increase in history: slogan:
any measure by the opposing party that resulted in increased revenues.

Greed: n.:
the motivating force behind modern society; the engine of Industry.

Green: n.:

1) the color associated with the environmental movement.

2) the color of putrefaction and decay; the hue of illness.

3) the color of money.

Greenmail: n.:
extortion in the boardroom; industrial piracy, where the treasure is not buried, but merely "sheltered."

Gresham's Law: n.:
"Bad money drives out good":
a broadly applicable principle of human conduct, equally true when applied to politics, religion, laws, etc.

Grief: n.:
the emotion of absence. Not, as it is practiced by those Americans of northern European ancestry, absence of emotion.

Grinch: proper name:
a sour character whose jealousy of other people's joy leads him to seek to take away the sources of that joy.
The original was a character in a children's book by Dr. Seuss.

Gubernatorial: adj.:
pertaining to a large frog in a small pond.

Guilt: n.:
natural secretion of the conscience gland. The fuel which the fires of religious devotion burn.

Gullible: adj.:
qualified for membership in the Great Electorate.

Gun: n.:

1) a metallic demon which skulks about seeking innocent bystanders to murder.

2) a popular scapegoat to the Left for failed social policies.

3) Colonel Colt's Patent Equalizer.

Guru: n.:
holy teacher. From the roots "goo" a sticky, slimy substance, and "roo" a creature with a deep pocket.

H

Habit: n.:
: the autopilot of the mind.
Bierce characterizes habit as shackles for the free. The Church calls nuns' clothing habits.

Hack: n.:
: a writer whose works do not appeal to my prejudices.
  v.t.:
in computerese, to do surgery on an ailing computer program with the delicacy of a woodchopper and the finesse of a cab driver.

Hallucination: n.:
: a vision not prescribed by my religion.

Hallucinogen: n.:
: a psychoactive agent lacking an effective lobby or press campaign.

Handbasket: n.:
: preferred conveyance to Hell. Travel to be along a road paved with good intentions, no doubt.

Handicapped: adj.:
in horse racing, carrying an extra burden. This practice intends to bring the performance of the best animals down to the level of the poorest, in order to maximize the take at the pari-mutuel windows.

Handsome: adj.:
the masculine of pretty.

Handwriting: n.:
the device we use to disguise our thoughts and feelings from others when a computer isn't available.

Hangover: n.:
1) second term administration.

2) conscience with teeth.

Harangue: n.:
an opponent's exhortation to his followers.
Bierce characterizes such a speaker as an "harangue-outang"; this is insulting to the Old Man of the Forest.

Harem: n.:
Big Rock Candy Mountain for adolescent males.
An institution in which women are supported in relative ease and luxury by a powerful man, in return for dramatically less service than would be required of them by a much poorer husband, lover or master. Execrated by men who believe they would never be able to afford one and by women who believe they would never be able to qualify to be selected for one.

Hastert: proper name:
Chicago Liberal slang which translates as "Menace."

Hatch: n.:
opening into a (usually odious and/or odious) lower domain.
    v.t.:
bring to fruition a potential enterprise, e.g., a plot or scheme.

Hatfield: proper name:
the real McCoy among western senators.

Hatred: n.:
the warm feeling we have for others who have bested us.

Haute: adj.:
a French term most easily translated as "overpriced."

Hawk: n.:
one of the political birds, long with dove, peacock, (Jim) crow and turkey. Notably absent from the list is the owl.

"He started it": clause:
I got caught doing it.

Head: n.:
1) the center of action of thought;
2) the goal for action when going to the bathroom.

Head shop: n.:
a retail establishment whose clientele are largely in need of new heads, having burned out their old ones.

Health: n.:
the stalking horse chosen by the abstemious to coerce us to their style of life, since they have worn out the soul for that use.
Good health is no more than the slowest and most comfortable way of dying.

Hearsay: n.:
the category of evidence which stands in support of the adage "talk is cheap."

Heart: n.:
1) the most metaphoric of the organs.
2) the haven at the end of the way through a man's stomach.

3) fashionable sleeve wear, among Romantics.

Heaven: n.:
venue of the afterlife for me and my friends; the carrot offered by religion. Variously described: as an abode of continuous delight where you go; as the deadly dull place where the "good" go; as the great cathouse in the sky where Muslims go.

Heavenbound: adj.:
hogtied by the dictates of politically powerful and socially conservative religions.

Hedonism: n.:
Live fast, love hard, die young and leave a fashionable corpse.

Hell-bent for election: adj.:
description of the candidate opposed by the religious right.

Hell's Bells: n.:
the phone, doorbell or alarm on the morning after.

Hellfire: n.:
half the stock in trade of the snake oil salesman who sells from a pulpit. Sold as a gift to one's neighbors, especially those who don't attend the sales meetings.

Hereafter: n.:
topic of conversation among dating youth.
Couple at the local lovers' lane:
"Let's talk about the hereafter."
"What do you mean?"
"Well, if you're not hereafter what I'm hereafter, you're going to be hereafter I'm gone."

Hermaphrodite: n.:
the traditional bisexual built for two.
A hermaphrodite must be a good thing: if it were a bad thing, it would have been renamed himmaphrodite.

Hero: n.:
traditionally, someone who didn't believe that what needed doing was valiant or glorious, but did it anyway.
A new variety is the "authentic American hero;" he is a serving government or military officer who sells lethal weapons to a country at war with his own in order to circumvent laws he is sworn to uphold. In a harsher, less enlightened age there was a different word for such men. Benedict Arnold, at least, never delivered.
One side's hero is the other side's traitor, or villain, if you're still into melodrama.

High moral ground: n.:
the position I attribute to the politician whose pronouncements most nearly match my prejudices.

Higher consciousness: n.:
greater state of inebriation.

Higher than a kite: adj. phrase:
for Charlie Brown, Ziggy or Thor, anywhere above the waist.

Highway robbery: n.:
"Speed Limit Strictly Enforced".

Hindenburg: proper name:
until the advent of the Republican Revolution in Talk Radio, the best known flaming Nazi gasbag.

Hip joint: n.:
sensamilla cigar.

Hippie: n.:
spiritual child of the Beat generation; the social (anti-social?) phenomenon of the '60s. Middle-aged spread has given the old term a whole new, less attractive, meaning.

"His name is mud": phrase:
: euphemistic expression of disapproval; the euphemism comes from the bowdlerization of the original "merde."

History: n.:
: the study of the actions of old white men. This is primarily due to the fact that most of what is worth studying was done by white men, though most of them were fairly young at the time.
: History is the account left by the victors. Historically, the few who have beaten out the Europeans have had other interests afterward than making marks on pieces of pressed wood pulp.

Hitler: epithet:
: anyone successful whose policies are more authoritarian and less liberal than mine.

Hockey: n.:
: a spectator sport popular among those who decry the increase of violence in the streets.

Holistic medicine: n.:
: the patient performs the cure and the doctor sends him the bill.
: Physicians use the term as a marketing ploy to make their practice sound more contemporary or "caring."
: Non-physicians use the term on the theory that practicing "holistic medicine" does not require a license to practice "medicine."
: If you see it spelled "wholistic," run, do not walk, to the nearest exit.

Hollywood: proper name:
: erstwhile spiritual capitol of California (the famed land of fruits and nuts), before the rise of Orange County.

Holocaust: n.:
: a term liberally applied to any situation involving death or repression in order to garner shock or sympathy. The term is not conservatively

applied, since the arch conservatives deny that there was ever any event for the term to refer to.

Hologram: n.:
a phenomenon with the semblance of reality, but lacking in substance, rather like the integrity of a politician or the honesty of a lawyer.

Holonym: n.:
a phrase contrived as the (fictitious) prototype for a catchy acronym. Originally, acronyms were used in order to save on syllables—TNT vs. tri-nitro toluene, RADAR vs. Radio Detection And RAnging, etc. In later use, evocative terms were coined to represent projects, political stances, etc., then the holonyms were coined to justify the marketable "acronyms." The practice of holonymy has not been recognized or sanctioned, yet, by other lexicographers.

Holy: adj.:
1) holier than thou.
more important to me than your life.

The Holy Land: n.:
any geographic division that has experienced religious warfare continuously for more than 1000 years.
Hang in there, Ireland.

Home: n.:
"Anywhere you hang your hat is home." Which explains why congressmen keep hatracks in their offices in their home districts: it's as close to keeping a home there as most of them ever get.

Homogenized: adj.:
having had all of the identifying, or interesting, characteristics removed.

Homophobia: n.:
cultural symptom of a pasture-ized mind.

Homophone: n.:
bane of the undereducated; multiple spellings for a single sound is simply too much to bear—or is that to much to bare?
The raw material from which most puns are constructed.
There is no truth to the assertion that a homophone is a telecommunications instrument rented from the Greenwich Village office of NYNEX.

Homosexual: n.:
one who takes the dictum "All flesh consorteth according to kind, and a man will cleave with his like" as other than apocryphal.
Popular scapegoat to the right for the failure of repressive child rearing practices.
For some reason, the term as a noun seems to be applied almost exclusively to males.
    adj.:
descriptive of a person who finds attractive those with whom they share common interests, tastes, genitalia...

Homosexual agenda: n.:
a political campaign, developed by the Third Reich and perpetuated by some of their social successors, that uses popular fear of variant sexual practice as a pretext for ignoring civil rights and other social guarantees.

Honest: adj.:
(of a politician) not yet caught.
(of a lawyer) retired.
(of an acquaintance) only inclined to tell those lies about me that I care to hear.

Honor: v.t.:
how a politician treats an offer to buy him.
    n.:

1) an archaic quality of behavior, which has survived primarily as a term of address: "Yes, your Honor."

2) that laudable element of the behavior of others that furthers my ends.

Honorable: adj.:

1) on, or aligned with, my side.

2) a title conferred on legislators and other governmental functionaries in yet another triumph of hope over experience.

Hood: n.:

1) the wool the executioner pulls over your eyes.

2) criminal who works by force rather than by guile.

When a candidate invites you to "under the hood," the options are not marvelous.

Hope: v.i.:

partake of junk food for the soul.

n.:

a broken promise of things to come.

Hops: n.:

a night-blooming aromatic from whose fermented juice we derive six-packs, keggers, microbrews, and other joys of life.

Hors d'oeuvres: n.:

an obscure French term which, from its conventional English pronunciation, must have something to do with the difference between stallions and geldings.

Horse's mouth: n.:

euphemistic attribution for a Washington information source.

Yet another illustration of how the Press get things all turned around.

Hospice: n.:
a place where you can get most of the care of a hospital without the intrusiveness. Where the terminally ill go so they can die without tubes and machines intervening.
Also, a similar level of care offered in the home.

Hostage: n.:
preferred currency for buying TV prime time exposure.

Hostel: n.:
a sort of hotel where the service is do-it-yourself.
The phenomenon of the Youth Hostel is a mystery: have you ever looked at a teenager's room?

Hot: adj.:
1) popular;
2) stolen.

Hot button: n.:
one that when pushed causes your face to turn red and your breath to go all funny.

House: n.:
establishment of ill-repute; as houses of Congress, House of Representatives.
As Polly Adler is said to have observed, it takes a heap of loving to make a home a house.

A house divided against itself cannot stand: adage:
in paraphrase, inspiration for the doctrines of the Church: a man divided against himself cannot withstand...

Hug: n.:
new-age panacea for human ills. If offered or solicited in the workplace, by a man, sexual harassment.

Human: adj.:
   unnatural.
      n.:
   a person belonging to my ethnic group. No others need apply.
Human error: n.:
   the cause of any catastrophe we can't blame on a machine.
Humility: n.:
   that trait in which the abstemious take the most pride.
Humor: n.:
   the name we choose to cloak our aggressions; polemic garlanded with punch lines.
Humorous: adj.:
   designed or intended to draw forth one or more of the traditional humors: blood, sweat, tears, etc.
Humpty-Dumpty: proper name:
   lexicographer to politicians, advertisers and activists.
Hunchback of Notre Dame: n.:
   key player in the Fighting Irish' new football formation.
   "I don't know him, but he's a dead ringer for Fra…"
Hunger strike: n.:
   (nominally) adult version of "I'm going to hold my breath until I turn blue and then you'll be sorry."
Hurricane: n.:
   natural State of the Union speech.
Hyde: proper name:
   Dr. Jackal on the Hill.
Hype: v.t.:
   sell by the use of exaggeration, with an extravagance of superlatives.

This is the alternative style to negative advertising in political campaigns.

Hyperbole: n.:
the staple from which the fabric of advertising is knit.
"Sell the sizzle, not the steak."
This leads naturally to the question "Where's the beef?"

Hypnopedia: n.:
prevalent activity in a college lecture hall on Monday morning.

Hypnotic: adj.:
having the same salutary effect on attention as a glowing cathode ray tube.

Hypochondria: n.:
a disease characterized by good health and general boringness; a common affliction of the rich and the lonely.

Hypochondriac: n.:
a patient who has been in failing health, typically, since before their doctor began his practice.

Hysteria: n.:
commodity dispensed by demagogues; standard reaction to a press campaign to create a new crisis.
little-known Muse: the patroness of patriotic rallies and demagogues worldwide.

Hysterical pregnancy: n.:
laboring under a misconception...

I

I: proper name:
   the center of the known universe.

"I don't do windows": phrase:
   Macintosh owners' mantra.

IRA: abbrev.:
   a real killer of a place to invest your money.

Iambic pentameter: n.:
   the dialect spoken by Shakespearian actors.

Iatrogenic: adj.:
   caused by the action of a doctor; as iatrogenic injury, from mistake or malpractice; iatrogenic disease, caught in the hospital; or iatrogenic penury, from lapse of health insurance.
   Not applicable to hypochondria, which is caused by the existence of doctors.

Ice cream: n.:
   the desirable nutritive component of milk.

Ideologue: n.:
   appointee by the other party.

Ideology: n.:
a body of beliefs, values, priorities advanced by the other side.

Idiom: n.:
ideophonic idiosyncrasy.

Idiosyncrasy: n.:
eccentricity in someone with status.

Idiot: n.:
anyone dumber than my in-laws.

Idle: adj.:
not currently making money.
The Idle Rich do not need to make money—they have people to do that for them; the Idle Poor can't make money—either they can't get jobs or the cost of keeping the job is as great as the pay.

Idolatry: n.:
fandom not condoned by my church.

"If we can send a man to the moon…": plaint:
when we sent men to the moon, the players and decision makers were engineers, technicians and scientists, and the bean counters were not in charge. The players in your pet project are lawyers, politicians and activists and they spend dollars to manage cents worth of useful applications.

"If you're so rich, why ain't you smart?": saying:
a national question derived from observation of American foreign policy.

"If you're so smart, why aren't you rich?": saying:
question from someone who read and actually believed *The Bell Curve*.

Ignoramus: n.:
member of the largest subclass of the human species.

Ignorance: n.:
a stubborn refusal to embrace beliefs that I hold strongly.

Ill-advised: adj.:
inclined to act in a manner contrary to my interests.

Illusion: n.:
something that is not what it seems, as when a lawyer seems to speak candidly to the jury, or a politician seems to hold certain popular views or values.

Illusory: adj.:
all smoke and no fire, as the violence in exhibition wrestling, or the relief you are likely to get from the newest tax reduction bill.

Illustration: n.:
what must be provided when the answer to "do I have to draw you a picture?" is "yes."

Illustrative: adj.:
showing my position in its best and most acceptable light.

Image: n.:
false image.

Imagination: n.:
the father of invention.

Immediately: adv.:
eventually.

Immoral: adj.:
unwilling to abide by my moral values.

Immortal: adj.:
having built a reputation, or a fortune, large and strong enough to last more than one generation after one's death.

Immortality: n.:
cancer of the whole body; the reward for a life of self-punishment, as promised by all Western religions.

Impairment: n.:
a decrease in ability to function in driving, created by alcohol and used as justification for magic numbers in drunk-driving laws. Decrease in ability to function in driving due to paraplegia, quadriplegia, infirmity, prescription drugs, hearing loss, or using a cellular phone is not to be considered as impairment.

Imperceptible: adj.:
demonstrating the salient characteristic of the typical non-executive pay raise.

Imply: v.t.:
accuse by indirection, when you don't have evidence to support the accusation or are afraid to make it openly and risk the reply.

Impolite: adj.:
inconvenient to me.

Important: n.:
self-important.

Imposing: adj.:
big; occasionally, expensive.

Impossible: adj.:
1) sufficiently inconvenient that I'm disinclined to do it.
2) beyond my understanding of how to do it.

Impoverished: adj.:
facing the morning of April 16.

Impractical: adj.:
requiring that I give up some of my authority, autonomy or wealth.

Impregnable: adj.:
   on the Pill.

Impressionable: adj.:
   susceptible to the wiles of the opposition. Susceptibility to my side's wiles is, of course, acumen, or maturity, if in reference to the young.

Improper: adj.:
   held, espoused, maintained or practiced by the other side.

Impromptu: adj.:
   performed without rehearsal, sometimes even without a script.

Improvisation: n.:
   "This isn't the way this was supposed to happen."

Improvise: v.i.:
   if you don't know it, dazzle them with your fancy footwork.

Impure: adj.:
   the condition of food and drink before the Government interceded to protect our precious bodily fluids, or of thoughts enticed by things not sanctioned by the church.

In God We Trust: motto:
   everyone else has let us down.
   Jean Shepard finishes it: "all others pay cash."

"In like Flynn": phrase:
   securely placed, comfortable, and contented; a tribute to the prowess of a Depression-era movie star.

In spite of: phrase:
   "This isn't what I intended to happen."

In The Mood: phrase:
   favorite song and sentiment of the 40's.
   The baby boom happened in the 40's.

Inane: adj.:
ready for prime-time.

Inauguration: n.:
a formal occasion derived from the old Roman practice of divining the future by putting their hands into the innards of sacrificed animals. The current practice is more in the nature of putting their hands into our soon-to-be-sacrificed wallets.

Incense: v.t.:
get right up my nose.

Incest: n.:
sibling revelry; a sport the whole family can enjoy.
Traditionally, the regional pastime of the Ozarks and Appalachia. Remember: the family that lays together stays together—generation after generation.

Inch: v.i.:
move one-ninth of the distance it would take to please a lady.

Income tax: n.:
a scheme that adds the burden of caring for the non-productive to that of keeping a job.

Incompatibility: n.:
motivation of the office wife; job description of the lady of the evening.

Inconceivable: adj.:
post-vasectomy.

Incongruous: adj.:
composed of inharmonious elements. Derived with minor respelling from "In Congress Assembled…"

Inconsistent: adj.:
the nature of behavior in the absence of rationality.

For example, TV news programs show rear views of nudists, but bleep the word "ass" from an interview with an athlete.

Incorrigible: adj.:
(too) easily encouraged.

Increase: n.:
growth: the mode of change of taxation, regulation, population, pollution, waistline, cancer, heart-disease rate and other indicators of civilization.
Growth is the *sine qua non* of business philosophy.

Incumbent: n.:
the candidate whose hand already knows the way into the till.

Indecent: adj.:
enticing; exciting; interesting.

Indecision: n.:
the mechanism by which we protect ourselves from having to take responsibility for the consequences of making errors of commission; the preferred path to procrastination.

Independence: n.:
the state of having forsworn allegiance and abrogated debt.

Independent: adj.:
having concealed allegiances.

Indifference: n.:
that emotion engendered in us by others' suffering.

Indigenous: adj.:
pertaining to those people living in an area before it was discovered by humans.

Inert: adj.:
exhibiting the degree of ambition and animation of a brother-in-law.

Inexorable: adj.:
out of control.

Inevitable: adj.:
fairly likely.

Infantry: n.:
the part of the army that marches on its stomach, especially into combat.

Infer: v.t.:
imply.
Infer and its complement imply were equated in the notorious *Merriam-Webster's New International Unabridged Dictionary, Third Edition*, igniting a holy war between Prescriptivists and Descriptivists.

Infinity: n.:

1) the next number larger than the largest countable number; hence, any number too large to visualize, like the number of grains of sand, the number of stars, the National Debt.

2) a brand of car that gained notoriety by the artifice of having their introductory series of commercials not show the product. They were artistically and tastefully done and therefore stood out sharply from their competition.

Inflammatory rhetoric: n.:
the programming content of C-Span, where it alternates with soporific bombast.
Liberals believe that speech incites violence, but not sex, while conservatives hold to the opposite view.

Inflation: n.:
Economy's disincentive for hiding money away in banks.

Influenza: n.:
debilitating, sometimes fatal, disease named for its similarity of symptoms and effect to the effect on the Body Politic of influence peddling. From the Italian.

Information: n.:
misinformation. The government relies on peoples' belief "if it's in black and white, it's right" to make it work.
Forunately, weather forecasters have broken the public of the belief that anything from a computer must be true and exact.

Information age: n.:
usually just far enough out of date to be less than completely useful.

Information Superhighway: n.:
1) unfortunate metaphor for electronic publishing. To extend the metaphor, most of the populace are using horse and buggy and just discovering bicycles; a fourth of them haven't mastered shoes yet.
2) the road less travelled. The New Age Bypass, aka the Misinformation Superhighway, gets the bulk of the traffic and nearly all of the press, which it shares with the Disinformation Alternate Route—the one that winds down among the bullrushes.

Informed electorate: n.:
1) the voting citizens of Utopia.
2) the worst nightmare of the professional politician and his campaign manager.

Informed sources: n.:
people who are ashamed to have their names attached to the drivel they're feeding the press.

Inlaw: n.:
one related by marriage and therefore not of significance for determining genetic relationship patterns, except in the Bible Belt.

Insane: adj.:
unable to tell right from wrong, but not currently holding office.
The general populace consists primarily of those who are dangerously insane and those who are not dangerous.

Inscrutable: adj.:
having the dastardly ability to act in other ways than I think I would in the same predicament.

Insecure: adj.:
unwilling to accept responsibility for their own values and opinions, so that they must justify themselves by declaring their tastes to be constants of the Universe.

Insensible: n.:
exhibiting the same empathy as does the conservative to the sufferings of the poor.

Insensitive: adj.:
(of a male) incapable of reading (usually female) minds.

Insight: n.:
legal inside information.

Insomnia: n.:
a medical condition easily treated by adminstration of a State of the Union address or its Opposition rebuttal.

Insurance: n.:
a legal game of chance where the house gets to set the bets and make up the rules.
Insurance companies set rates based on the number of accidents, then refuse to insure the 10 percent of people who are responsible for 50 percent of the accidents.
It's hard to feel sorry for the tribulations of an industry that can spend billions of dollars a year on advertising, pay sizable dividends

to its holders, then weep that regulation makes it impossible for them to be profitable.

Intellectual rights: n.:
a tautology: any discussion of rights is pretty much an intellectual exercise, divorced from the real world.

Intelligence: n.:
ability to score high on a test designed to predict how successful one would be likely to be in the turn-of-the-century French Civil Service and updated to include conformance with white American cultural norms.

Intelligent: adj.:
bright enough to agree with me.

Intelligentsia: n.:
a class who think that because they spend all their time playing with words they have the right to control the definitions.

Intemperate: adj.:
tending to act before I have time to make up my mind about how it should be done.

Intensity: n.:
that property that distinguishes the great from the good, the devotee from the dilettante.
Intensity is perhaps the most difficult trait for the actor to simulate.

Intensive care: n.:
expensive care.

Interest: n.:
1) the ability to hold attention.
2) the ability to draw the attention of bankers.

Interest rate: n.:
the tool used to balance supply and demand in the money markets. It is a tool with all the precision and delicacy of a bulldozer.

Interfere: v.i.:
create noise and suppress intelligible content.

Interference: n.:
activity that does not forward my goals.

Internalize: v.t.:
treat in accordance with Stout's *Anglo-Saxon Theory of Emotions and Dessert:* freeze them and hide them in the belly.

Internet: proper name:
the hose that will fuel the Information Revolution; or extinguish it. Its reputation, if not its shape, is extraordinarily hyperbolic.

Interpret: v.t.:
change the language, or the meaning of.
Often said of a judge's actions toward the law or the Constitution.

Interview: n.:
the journalist's revenge on the prominent and powerful.

Intestine: n.:
that region of the body where we thoughtfully convert our food into sustenance for plants.

Intimidate: v.t.:
teach the facts of life.

Intolerable: adj.:
mildly inconveniencing or vaguely offensive.

Intolerance: n.:
1) a really good movie;
2) a really bad social policy.

Intolerant: adj.:
exhibiting the love, caring and empathy characteristic of any Western religion.

Intransigent: adj.:
unwilling to accept the generous compromise I have offered.

Introspection: n.:
a period of observation in the most interesting and important of surroundings.

Invention: n.:
the daughter of Necessity and Imagination; exalted patroness of Culture.

Inventory: n.:
a mysterious demon that sits on shelves in the warehouse and steals profits from the company that has evoked it.

Inverse: adj.:
a relation between two things such that, as one becomes greater, the other becomes lesser, *e.g.*, the relationship between competence and confidence.

Inversion layer: n.:
Mother Nature's attempt to put a lid on an area to keep the pollution inside and away from the non-polluters.

Irate: adj.:
adjectival form pertaining to the occupants of the Emerald Isle and their descendants.

Ireland: proper name:
the nation named for an emotion.

Irony: n.:
when Fate sucker punches you.

Irrelevant: adj.:
not in support of my position.

Irresponsible: adj.:
acting after the fashion of the Press dealing with an important story that has no fast-breaking information to carry it through its obligatory daily exposure.

Irreverent: adj.:
not inclined to show adequate respect for me or my positions.

Isolate: v.t.:
a time-honored verb which the medical research community made into a noun. The International Standards Organization has now extended its range to include adjective; 9000 times an adjective.

Itinerary: n.:
schedule for a travelogue.

Ivory tower: n.:
an institution, expensive, delicate, beautiful and utterly lacking utility in or ability to withstand the workaday world.

J

Jackal: n.:
a denizen of the jungle noted for his forthright and straightforward relationships with the top elements of the animal hierarchy: sort of an independent prosecutor of the animal kingdom.

Jaundiced: adj.:
the appropriate color of eye to compensate for the rose-colored visions of demagoguery

Jazz: n.:
"If you have to ask what jazz is, you'll never know." Louis Armstrong's description makes it the perfect exemplar for most of the Twentieth Century.

Jealousy: n.:
that emotion kindled in us by observation of a loved one's independent happiness or success.

Jewels: n.:
a woman's most prized possessions, be they precious or family. Either will evoke territoriality and pride of ownership.

Jitterbug: n.:
once-popular dance whose fans have gone on to condemn the lewdness of rock-and-roll dancing.

Job: n.:
the activity which we attend to achieve our daily bread. Named for a character in the Bible in recognition of his pioneering of the lifestyle.

Jock: n.:
a subclass of athlete; nominally, a strapping physical specimen, with more muscle than anything else in its head; jerk.

Joe Camel: proper name:
90's incarnation of John Barleycorn.

Joe Six-pack: proper name:
great-grandson of Everyman.

Joint session of Congress: n.:
1) a little boo in the Cloakroom.
2) one wag's characterization of the hearings on Marijuana Law reform.

Joust: n.:
medieval equivalent of the modern morning commute.

Judicial hearing: n.:
the legal profession's response to the medical condition of insomnia.
    oxymoron:
they say justice is blind; they didn't mention the deficiencies in the other senses.

Juggler: n.:
one in training to become an accountant.

Juice: v.t.:
extract the inner fluids from.

Junket: n.:
a paid vacation for the man on the public payroll.

Junta: n.:
government of the people, by the Army, for the generals.

Jury: n.:
the lynchpin of the American legal system.

Just: adj.:

1) barely;

2) fair, equitable and merciful.
It's sometimes amazing how much a language can reveal about its society.

Just In Time: adj. phrase:
a management scheme that ensures that any problems with suppliers will be passed along to the customer.

Just Say No: slogan:
except to me.

Justice: n.:
retribution; ritualized vengeance.
Two wrongs that make a right, so long as my side gets to commit the second one.

"Justice is blind:" phrase:

1) Dame Justice is shown blindfolded. This is because she is so ashamed of the way "justice" is dealt with—and dealt—in these days.

2) Republican accusation against the Reno Justice Department.

"Justice was served": phrase:
on a silver platter; to the highest bidder.

"Justice was not served": phrase:
conventional denial of the fact that real justice is self serving. This contrasts with Justices, who are frequently self-serving.

Juvenile: adj.:
old enough to do the crime, young enough to dodge the time. Juvenile justice runs very close to being an oxymoron.

K

Kaleidoscope: n.:
the instrument that inspired the first two generations of computer art.

Kangaroo court: n.:
a body who have declared themselves a quorum assembled for the practice of Judge Lynch's law.

Kemp: n.:
inferior hairs mixed in with those of quality in order to cheapen the blend.

Keystone cops: n.:
Pennsylvania police, especially Philadelphia, Pennsylvania.

Kiddie porn: n.:
depictions of children in sexual or suggestive contexts, unless funded or presented by a large corporation catering to Middle America.

Kidney: n.:
one of a pair of swimming-pool shaped organs which filter the yellow color and the bad smells from the blood.

"Kids nowadays": phrase:
the oldest known complaint still in regular use. It may even be older than some of the jokes still in regular use.

A popular diatribe on the ill manners and bad attitudes of the younger generation is revived periodically; it is attributed to Socrates. This leads one to wonder if the Athenians had developed the institution of deficit spending.

Killer bees: n.:
the latest in a series of conscriptions from Africa to the New World.

King: n.:
a ruler appointed by God, or by the Committee to Reelect the President, depending on historical period.

Kit: n.:
a collection of the components necessary to create a manufactured item. Usually delivered with one or two parts missing and with the dread words "Some Assembly Required."

Kite: n.:
a flying machine which cannot be successfully operated by the hero of a daily comic strip.

Kleptomaniac: n.:
an addicted thief who steals for the love of theft rather than for gain.

Knapp: v.t.:
to create scars on the hands and fingers while trying to make rocks into stone tools after the fashion of the ancients.

Knee: n.:
the organ of supplication.

Knee-jerk: adj.:
reacting without thought or consideration; substituting jingle and sound-bite for thought.

Knot: n.:
a blemish that is attractive in a pine board, but not on the side of your head.

Know thyself: dictum:
when used in the biblical sense, an insult.

Knowledge: n.:
the residuum of experience, if you were paying attention at the time. Frequently confused with intelligence, mostly by those who are deficient in both.

Knuckle: n.:
sandwich makings for the rowdy.

Koran: n.:
the Newer Testament.

Ku Klux Klan: proper name:
early conservative PAC of the Old South, named for the sound of a rifle's action cycling; and about equally compassionate.

Kumquat: n.:
citrus fruit known primarily as the butt of jokes in '30s movie comedies.

L

Labor: n.:

1) the loyal opposition to Management in the government of Industry.

2) the hard-work part of making babies.

A young mother to be, worried about labor pain, asked her mother for a description.

"Take your lower lip with both hands and pinch it as hard as you can."

The daughter did this and said "Well, that's not too bad. I think I can take that."

Her mother nodded and said "Do it again. Now, stretch it over your head and staple it to the back of your neck."

Labor-saving: adj.:

capital-expending.

Lag: v.i.:

be slow, as the government in implementing promised tax reductions.

Laissez faire: n.:
French for license to steal.

Lampoon: n.:
satire in baggy pants.

Landslide victory: n.:
any win by my side that did not require a recount. Though, the way modern campaigns are run, mudslide would be a more appropriate term.

Language: n.:
the principal barrier to communication.

Laocoön: proper name:
a Greek who, with his sons, got involved with the Attic version of red tape.

Larceny: n.:
the motivating force of Commerce.
It comes in 3 major categories:
1) petty larceny, the theft of items of small value,
2) grand larceny, theft measured in $1000 increments, and
3) Gary Larson-y, theft of cows.

Lares and penates: n.:
Roman entities who fulfilled the functions now performed by the dog, the automobile and the television set.

Laryngitis: proper name:
famous Greek adventurer, noted for his breathy, raspy voice.

Laughter: n.:
the most socially acceptable excuse for bad manners.

Law: n.:
1) the body of rules that the elite have established for the rest of us to live by.

2) the profession dedicated to circumvention to the body of rules…

Law and Order: n. phrase:
a political movement that co-opts the press to create an anti-crime hysteria in order to justify institution of restrictive laws and centralization of power.
I lay down the Law to keep you in Order.
Two of the most successful Law and Order candidates of the Twentieth Century were Adolph Hitler and Richard Nixon.

"The law is an ass": maxim:
a popular misapprehension, probably originated from watching lawyers.

Lawsuit: n.:
America's favorite participation sport to be played out in public. It seems to be the aspiration of half the nation to become a professional.

Lawyer: n.:

1) a common misspelling; cf. LIAR.

2) one trained in circumvention of the Law. Ambrose Bierce defined lawyer as "one skilled in circumvention of the law." Observation would indicate that skill is not required.

Animal rights groups have suggested that the use of laboratory animals be supplanted by the use of lawyers, which would produce several advantages:

1) lawyers breed faster;

2) laboratory personnel are less likely to form emotional attachments to lawyers;

3) even using threats and bribery, there are some things you just can't get a rat to do.

Lawyers work on the back side of the Golden Rule: they make the rules so they can get the gold. In this mode, they are called "legislators."

Lay: n.:
lie. Except when someone is sent out to "get the lay of the land."

Lazy: adj.:
disinclined to perform unnecessary work and disagreeing with me as to what work is necessary.

Leader: n.:
one whose reputation for kindness, generosity and trustworthiness is such that no one wants to have him behind them; hence, the position out front.

Leadership: n.:
the art of being a hindrance such that everyone is held up behind you.
A definitive characteristic of renowned executives.
A trait commonly claimed by politicians running for office.

Learn from another's mistakes: phrase:
a rare talent, occasionally found among those who also exhibit common sense. What we usually learn from others' mistakes is how to make them for ourselves.

Lebensraum: **n.:**
German for "elbow room." The Germans have notoriously expansive elbows.

Lecture: n.:
secular sermon. If you can't teach it, preach it, then you can say you've done your duty.
The collegiate antidote to the problem of insomnia.

Leech: n.:
a bloodsucking worm. Unlike the politician and lawyer, who share this definition, a leech may occasionally be of utility, in medicine.

Left: adj.:
opposite of right: to the conservative, wrong.

Left lane: n.:
that portion of the highway inhabited by the pickup, the luxury car, the motor home and the talker-on-cellular-phone.

Leg: n.:
a functional portion of the anatomy which women's fashions expose in direct proportion to the general health of the economy.

Legal: adj.:
permissible to the powers-that-be.

Legalese: n.:
a dialect carefully constructed so as to obfuscate and make ambiguous the laws under which we are required to live; the secret jargon of an elitist conspiracy to isolate the man in the street from the seats of power, and to separate him from as much as is feasible of his wealth.

Legally competent: adj phrase:
a term in the body of law used to refer to the mental capacity of someone other than a lawyer.

Legally defensible: adj phrase:
1) wealthy;
2) potentially profitable.

Legally responsible: adj phrase:
1) not an attorney;
2) not the client of a media-successful attorney;
3) not a member of a media-effective minority.

Legend: n.:
secular myth. Usually about events or persons of long ago, hence the importance of "a legend in his own time" as an accolade. A "legend in his own mind," the kind we most often see these days, is merely someone who thinks he's fabulous.

Legerdemain: n.:
a campaign statement or a lawyer's summation speech.

Legislated Morality: oxymoron:
what Congress offers us in lieu of moral legislators.

Legislature: n.:
an assemblage, mostly of lawyers, which sits for the purpose of promulgating laws which are so formulated as to ensure full employment for lawyers.
A puppet show, wherein the peformers rant and posture in response to the operation of their controlling strings by the owners of those strings (and puppets) or their appointed lobbyists.

Legitimate: adj.:
complying with that portion of the law with which I am in agreement.

Lei: n.:
the traditional greeting offered a visitor to the Pacific Islands; homonymous to the desired greeting of the bulk of the visitors.

Leisure: n.:
the class of activity that the Industrial Revolution, then the Atomic Age, then the Information Revolution, was supposed to make available to the Common Man. Another broken promise of things to come.

Lemming: n.:
a small Arctic rodent whose social patterns recall those of the party faithful or the truly devout.

Leper: n.:
one who elicits the same degree of acceptance and tolerance as a Liberal in the 104th Congress.

Lepidoptera: n.:
the order of insects whose adults are the prettiest and whose children are the most voracious, sort of a six-legged Jet Set.

Lesbian: n.:
a woman who carries a belief in the maxim "the best man for the job is a woman" into her private life.

Lese majeste: n.:
an offence against the wearer of the crown, as contrasted with treason, which is an offence against the office of the crown.

Less: n.:
more, written in Green ink.

Lesser: n.:
hopefully, the one of the evils who actually got elected.

Let's Make A Deal: proper name:
the official game show of Capitol Hill; the lobbyist's motto.

Level playing-field: n.:
one tilted my way.
The stated goal of trade negotiators (not to be confused with the actual goals of trade negotiators.)

Lever: n.:
Archimedes' world mover, lacking only its fulcrum to be functional.

Leveraged buyout: n.:
a form of corporate piracy wherein the plunder is the ammunition used in the attack.

Lewd: adj.:
showing more skin than I have the nerve (or body) to.

Lexicon: n.:
> high-status dictionary.

Lexicographer: n.:
> one who lays down the law in words.

Liability: n.:
> 1) anything serving as a handicap, burden or, especially before the law, expense: e.g., the Administration record, to a Vice President running for President.
>
> 2) the legal profession's substitute for responsibility.

Liaison: n.:
> an illicit affair. Note the presence of many "liaison officers" in any diplomatic embassy; is this the origin of the expression "foreign affairs?"

Libel: n.:
> reportage *a la* tabloid.

Liberal: n.:
> 1) one who believes any problem can be solved by drowning it in dollars—a few of his and a lot of everyone else's.
>
> 2) a former conservative, after his arrest.
>
> 3) one who believes any criminal can be rehabilitated, except an ex-Nazi or KKK member.
>
> 4) one who believes in freedom of speech as long as it doesn't offend anyone he feels guilty toward.
>
> 5) one guilty of crimes of compassion, to the eyes of the conservative.

Liberal Arts: n.:
> a field of study that enables one to get a college degree without having to be able to do math.

Liberal arts education: n.:
a term that, to the degree that it's not an oxymoron, refers to a program of college attendance focussed on the fields which emphasize argument over experiment and proof by assertion and obfuscation over proof by demonstration or analysis.

Liberal court: n.:
one which declines to impose as a legal obligation behaviors dictated by the spokesmen of the most conservative and repressive religious groups, limits the discretionary use of power by police agencies, or which imposes any punishment less than the most severe possible for any blue-collar, especially drug-related, crime.

Liberation: n.:
ritualized change of masters, usually by violence.

Libertine: n.:
a rascal who dares to enjoy his life more than I do mine.

Liberty: n.:
1) the First Lady of New York City.

2) license.

Library: n.:
an institution which has evolved from being the repository of the knowledge of a society to being a mausoleum for the forgotten ideas of prior generations—and the free point of entry to the Internet.

License: v.t.:
to sell a permit for the exercise of a liberty.
    n.:
lewd conduct.

License to kill: n.:
drinking-driver's license.

Lie: n.:
>the normal content of an advertisement, political speech or promise.
>v.i.:
>hide the truth.
>There are three major ways to lie:
>1) tell an untruth, or deny the truth;
>2) tell a partial truth in such a way as to lead to a false conclusion;
>3) tell the truth in such a way as to cause it to be disbelieved.

Lie, cheat and steal: phrase:
>the Holy Trinity of the professions of Law and Politics.

Life: n.:
>that brief, often painful, interlude between oblivion and eternity; excrement of the Gods.

Life insurance: n.:
>a game where you bet the underwriter that you won't live as long as he thinks you will. If you win, you can't collect.

Limbo: n.:
>1) Oblivion, the land of the oblivious. The place to which things of no value are relegated.
>2) the suburb of Hell where unbaptized souls are sent.

Linen: n.:
>bedding or towels, made of cotton or polyester.

Lion: n.:
>1) a large African cat whose normal posture is homonymous with his name.
>2) the creature who taught the IRS how to share.

Lion's share: n.:
>popularly, most; originally, all; practically, as much as he wants.

Literati: n.:
people who value literacy, but not numeracy, logic or duty; self-appointed arbiters of fashion, taste and style.

Literature: n.:
body of writing. The soul is poetry.

Litigation: n.:
the American national pastime.
One of the immediate causes of the American Revolution was the imposition of the Stamp Act, which primarily acted to impose a fee on the filing of lawsuits. This, of course, could not be borne.

Litter: n.:
the excrement of Economy.

"Live and learn": motto:
good advice if you plan on living very long.

Loaf: v.i.:
pursue the vocation of a brother-in-law.

Loan: n.:
all-purpose tool for creating alienation, destroying friendships, dismembering budgets, collapsing economies.

Lobby: n.:
the entry to a building, wherein the public can be detained to prevent their becoming involved in the conduct of the work going on inside.
    v.i.:
provide social welfare for employed legislators.

Lobbyist: n.:
oilcan to the machinery of government.
A lobbyist pays politicians to get them to make up their minds about how to make up their minds.

Lock: n.:
a device to help keep honest people honest.

Logarithm: n.:
the agency that allows adders to multiply.

Logic: n.:
a train of successive conclusions that leads to what I knew all along.

Logistic: adj.:
1) pertaining to logic.
2) pertaining to the transport and supply of the military.
Apparently another instance of a word with contradictory definitions.

Logorrhea: n.:
sitting and racing the mouth without engaging the brain.
Filibuster.

Logrolling: n.:
how the business of Congress gets moved when contributors haven't greased the ways adequately.

Logy: adj.:
as a stand-alone word, heavy, dull, slow; as a suffix, science or study of. Origin is related to the response of students to the presentation of science in the lecture hall.

Londonderry Air: n.:
tear gas.

Long arm of the law: phrase:
a traditional term left over from the days when most lawmen lived either in barracks or boarding houses.

Loose: v.t.:
lose.
    adj.:
the nature of the morals of anyone more successful in the dating game than I.

Loser: n.:
the kind of guy who could strike out at a womens' prison with a briefcase full of pardons.

Loser pays: adj.:
a legal policy designed to screw the victim, since she's shown she can't fight back effectively, anyway.

Loss: n.:
equal and opposite reaction to profit.
The emotion that is with us each and every day of our lives.

Lot: proper name:
an Old Testament hero, noted for escaping from the destruction of Sodom by sucking up to a couple of high-status religious visiting firemen.

Lott: proper name:
high-status legislator who cements his position by sucking up to Old-Testamentarian religious power brokers.

Lottery: n.:

1) legal numbers racket, usually with a payoff percentage a lot lower than anyone would tolerate in an illegal game.

2) the only tax paid by volunteers.

3) a tax on innumeracy.

Love: n.:

1) an institutionalized neurosis whereby we rationalize our desire to meddle in the lives of others.

2) the embers of passion.

    v.t.:

own.

As in "I love you. Take good care of yourself; you belong to me."

Love thy neighbor: credo:
lifestyle of suburbia in the 60's.

Lowest Common Denominator: n.:
quality standard for prime-time programming.

Luck: n.:
chance, when it grants us something we think we want.

Lucky dog: n.:
someone whom chance has handed something I desired.

Luddites: n.:
nineteenth century precursor of the Trial Lawyers Association. The Luddites destroyed machinery with sledges and explosives to protect their jobs; the lawyers destroy industries with writ and judgment to enhance their incomes.

Lung: n.:
a mechanism thoughtfully provided by a benevolent Nature to remove pollutants from the air.

Lust: n.:
that emotion that adds luster to life; the stuff daydreams are made of.

Luxury: n.:
one of the items that comes first in the typical budget.

Lynch: v.t.:
enforce order without benefit of law.
proper name:
the most widely emulated jurist in American history.

M

Macchiavellian: adj.:
describing a set of principles which explain why we should "put not our trust in princes."

Machismo: n.:
the game of "my balls are bigger than yours" with the pants left on. Basically a game of bluff.

Madam: n.:
she for whom the belles toil.

Madison Avenue: proper name:
purveyor of T&A to the masses of America; exporters to the world.
   adj.:
smarmy; insipid and in questionable taste.

Maddening: adj.:
having the emotional impact of a teenager, a do-gooder, or a reformed smoker.

Madness: n.:
a state often confused with genius by those who have neither.

Some are born mad, some achieve madness, some have madness thrust upon them.

Magic: n.:

1) since Clarke, any sufficiently advanced technology.

2) a belief system fostered by ingrained laziness.

We go to a witch to get a love philtre so that maid on the next farm will fall in love with us, and we won't have to do the hard things, like improve our breath, wash the manure from beneath our nails, bathe...

This same attitude pervades modern management: they believe that if they pay a consultant, put up a few posters, hold a couple of pep rallies and say a few magic buzzwords, their business will suddenly turn around and become successful without their having to do the hard work of changing the habits and management styles that created the trouble in the first place.

Maiden: n.:

a woman who has never been with child; often confused with virgin: a woman who has never tried to become with child.

Mainline: adj.:

right-wing recasting of "mainstream."

v.t.:

inject (illegal) drugs directly into the bloodstream to create instant gratification and maximum addictive effect.

Mainstream: n.:

where all the political pressure groups claim to stand.

v.t.:

1) create a population of largely ineducable students who cost ten times as much per capita to house as the youth around them cost to educate.

2) remove mentally ill people from the surroundings where they can get care and therapy and transfer the financial responsibility for them from the state to private agencies. Make homeless.

Majority: n.:
a term with multiple magical meanings in politics and the law:
1) the authority for a segment of a group to impose their will on the remainder, so long as they outnumber them. This practice seems to be derived from the traditional principle "God is on the side with the bigger battalions."
2) the date on which a child becomes an adult, thereby gaining the right to be drafted, to become liable in contracts, to buy tobacco or to vote, but not to drink.

Make one see reason: n.:
bully, browbeat or brainwash until they suscribe to my point of view.

Male: adj.:
privileged, pampered, violent, chauvinistic, blameworthy.

Malfeasance: n.:
action in office, improperly taken for personal gain.
Which is to say, nearly any official action.

Malpractice: n.:
action by a licensed professional that does not meet the expectations of the client—or, more to the point, of the client's lawyer.

Mammon: proper name:
ancient name for Dow Jones.

Mammon fodder: n.:
blood offering to the God of the MBA; generally offered up on the Altar of Short-Term Profits. The ritual is traditionally referred to a "downsizing" or "rightsizing" or a similar euphemism.

Manage: v.t.:
   once, to provide leadership and direction to an enterprise; now, to attend meetings, draft budgets and be late with performance reviews.

Managed trade: n.:
   a market where there are sheriffs to curtail some of the activities of the robber barons.

Management: n.:
   the petty aristocracy in the kingdom of Industry.

Manager: n.:
   all too often, one who has confused the worth of valuable contribution with that which is merely expensive.

Mandate: n.:
   an electoral plurality used as an excuse for imposing an ideology.

Manipulation: n.:
   the technique by which my opponent cynically plays on the fears and ignorance of the populace to trick them into supporting something I don't approve of.

Manners: n.:
   rituals for polite behavior; recorded and offered up in lieu of courtesy, which can only be taught by example.

Manslaughter: n.:
   murder without intent, *i.e.*, mindless violence.

Manure: n.:
   natural fertilizer; hence the custom of refering to the "fertile imagination" of the popular writer, filmmaker, artist, etc.

March: n.:
   special-interest parade, especially if not associated with a major holiday.

March Hare: proper name:
   cultural icon who evolved into the Easter Bunny.

Marijuana: n.:
a remarkable herb which has the ability to impair the mental functioning of those who campaign against its use.

Marionberry jam: n.:
a condiment much prized by the media of Washington, D.C. Please note, however, that no jar should be considered authentic unless it has a little crack.

Market: v.t.:
misrepresent, in hopes of attracting a larger audience.

Marketplace: n.:
from the left, the locus of greed, wickedness and impropriety; from the right, the appropriate arena for the endorsement of the values I agree with.

Marriage: n.:
the headstone of modern society.
According to Bierce, "The state or condition of a community consisting of a master, a mistress and two slaves, making in all, two."
The anodyne to the tribulation of libido.

Marshmallow: n.:
a confection noted for its consistency, the firmness of which evokes memories of American foreign policy.

Martian: n.:
the only language in which it is possible accurately to describe human emotion. Not spoken by humans.

Martyr: n.:
one who has deemed survival of my group to be of greater worth than survival of his individual; one who has shown the last full measure of his devotion to my cause.
If his action is not in support of my cause, he is not a martyr, but rather a fanatic, zealot or brainwashed dupe.

Marx: n.:
1) Karl, the prophet of Communism, of which Lenin was the messiah.
2) a family (Groucho, Chico, Harpo, Zeppo, Gummo) of comedians much revered by teenagers of the '30s and college students of the '60s.
3) a manufacturer of toys and electric trains, especially during the Depression and War years.

Marxism: n.:
a pipe-dream social system that believed that the proper function of the State was to work itself out of a job.

Masses: n.:
Marx's term for the labor force. Also "John Q. Public," *hoi polloi*, "the great unwashed." This last may account for Marxism's relative success in France.

Master: n.:
1) obsolete honorific for a boy, changing to Mister on his majority or marriage, whichever came first.
2) the one who delegates the blame when things go wrong.
adj.:
having overweening authority, as master key.
v.t.:
to gain a minimal competence at, as to master the guitar.

Masturbation: n.:
self-love brought to the physical arena; safest sex, free from risk of disease or pregnancy; giving yourself a helping hand. The only established danger is to the career aspirations of Surgeons General who publicly recognize it as a valid part of sexuality.

Matador: n.:
the most politically incorrect of Hemingway's sportsmen.

Mathematics: n.:
the hardest of the "hard sciences."
Traditionally, mathematicians have taken pride in the assertion that their work has no practical value or application. In recent times, statisticians and pollsters have come along to do the mathematicians proud.

Mature: adj.:
acting in a way that I approve of.
    v.i.:
experience adulteration of the spirit.

Maturity: n.:
a character trait attributed to children and authority figures. The children seem to lose it at about age 5, not to regain it until their children have 5-year-olds of their own. The attribution to authority figures is a courtesy representing yet another triumph of hope over experience.

Mausoleum: n.:
apartment house for the afterlife.

maxim: n.:
a helping of wisdom small and sweetened enough to be swallowed and digested at one sitting.

MBA: n.:
the badge of the enemy, to technical types at least, in the war to improve competitiveness.

Measure: n.:
assign such numbers to as will advance my position.

Mechanics: n.:
a code word that physicists use to tell you that you're not going to like it:

Orbital mechanics: to speed up, slow down; to slow down, speed up.

Quantum mechanics: everything is a wave and a particle; if you know where it's going, you can't tell where it is and if you know where it is, you can't tell where it's going; you can't tell whether time is running forward or backward.

Statistical mechanics: the three laws of thermodynamics; there are no perpetual motion machines.

Media representative: n.:
1) a reporter who has better name recognition than the subject they're interviewing.
2) a reporter putting on airs.

Mediator: n.:
one who has parlayed a knack for getting caught in the middle into a high-status profession.

Medieval: adj.:
reminiscent of the times when the Church reigned supreme.

Medium: adj.:
not very good, not really bad. Plural *media*; reference news media, print media and now multimedia.

Medicine: n.:
that profession which, in treating those who are rich and healthy, strives to alleviate both conditions.

Meditation: n.:
masturbation of the mind.

Meek: adj.:
   appointed to inherit the earth.
   The way things have been going, this translates to "like a cockroach." This may account for the manners of many of the social groups that claim meekness (or the prophesied inheritance) for themselves.

Megalomania: n.:
   an offensive form of insanity which leads the victim to think he's better than I am.

Mein Kampf: book title:
   Contract With Germany.

Mein Kemp: book title:
   the story of a running mate.

Melancholic: adj.:
   variant of "melon-colic", the emotional state of a husband after enduring a "Honey, do" weekend.

Melancholy: n.:
   emotional state famous for its effect on babies and Danes.

Melting pot: n.:
   the all-purpose American metaphor.
   To the conservative, the cupel that refines the noble metal from the dross; to the liberal, the crucible wherein we improve the base metal by alloying.

Member: n.:
   anglicized *membrum virile*: penis; hence, the frequent reference to "the Honorable Member" in parliamentary debate.
   This also accounts for Death and Dismemberment being seen as equivalent.

Memory: n.:
recollection of past events, as filtered through our desires, prejudices and experiences; the closest most of us get to composing fiction in our everyday lives.

Mens sana in corpore sano: phrase:
Roman for glass ceiling: "the men's sauna is the corporate sauna" (women need not apply).

Mental: adj.:
this word comes to us from the Latin from two different directions: *mens*, mind and *mentum*, chin. This may explain why some people seem to think they look smarter by walking around with their chins up in the air. Anyone whose mind is such as to prompt him to lead with his chin is not leading from strength.

Mentally incompetent: adj phrase:
having demonstrated a dangerous propensity for coming to conclusions or expressing convictions at odds with my own.

Mercenary: n.:
one who has the temerity to charge me for doing what I would have him do.

Merchants of Death: *nou*n phrase:
medieval version of the military-industrial complex.

Mercury: n.:
1) a liquid metal commonly enclosed in glass tubes for measuring heat; hence, the heated dispositions of those affected by it.

2) the Roman patron deity of florists.

Mercy: n.:
an exclamation of dismay.

Message: n.:
the hidden meaning an action, especially an official action, but only the meaning that I want conveyed.
"We must send a message to ___ with this legislation. Repealing this law would send the wrong message..."

Meta-analysis: n.:
an activity that seeks to inject meaning retroactively into the published results of experiments. The purpose seems to be to allow publication without undergoing the tedium of running one's own experiments.

Metamorphosis: n.:
one verse of a poem by Ovid, a Roman poet named after eggs.

Metaphor: n.:
1) smokescreen.
Metaphors are conventionally used to disguise the fact that we do not understand something well enough to explain it accurately. When someone characterizes their presentation as a "metaphor for ___," look very closely for the man behind the curtain.

2) the recreational aspect of language.

Metempsychosis: n.:
not a very large psychosis, not a really small psychosis, just a metempsychosis.

Micromanage: v.t.:
interfere with the operation of; specify the solution down to the finest detail, without having any understanding of the problem.

Mid-East policy: myth:
"Don't tread on me! Oh! Well, don't do it again. Oh!..." *ad nauseam* and, seemingly, *ad infinitum*.

The traditional animosities in the Mid-East force a delicate balancing act between the pro-Jewish voting and contributing blocs on the one hand and the oil reserves and the money they create on the other.

Middle age: n.:
that awkward intermediate stage between the bitter cynicism of the young and the weary cynicism of the old.

Middle class: n.:
the touchstone of American politics; the grouping that everyone but the very rich and the welfare cheats is supposed to belong to.
Originally based on profession and social status, it is now used almost exclusively as an indicator of income: to the Republicans, $50,000 to $500,000 per year; to the Democrats, $10,000 to $100,000 per year.

Might: n.:
the raw material of right.

Militant: adj.:
aspiring to the violence of the Army, but not to the discipline.

Military: n.:
the next-to-last refuge of the scoundrel.
Which explains why so many politicians are retired military personnel.
    adj.:
a term used broadly for generating oxymorons, as: military intelligence, military preparedness, military justice…

Militia: n.:
irregular military. A well-regulated militia is necessary to the security of a free state; an unregulated militia is central to the insecurity of a political state.

Mind: v.i.:
be obedient or attentive; hence the phrase "Never mind" being so common in child rearing today.
  n.:
the skeleton which gives form to the emotional flesh of the soul.

Mindset: n.:
a marvelous double metaphor for the evolution of opinion:
a) decline, as in sunset;
b) congeal, as in the setting of concrete.

Minimum wage: n.:
the line that separates employment from slavery.

Miracle: n.:
an outcome I didn't expect but approve of anyway.

Miraculous: adj.:
the result of hard work, planning and preparation that I would have been unable or unwilling to perform; as a racing driver's "miraculous" survival of a crash.

Mirror: n.:
flame to the moth of Vanity.

Miscegenation: n.:
the final homage to the dictum "variety is the spice of life." Laws forbidding miscegenation have been common in Christian nations; their only positive value would be that they enable hybrid vigor in the products of their violation; the presence of such laws only encourages violation.

Misery: n.:
subjugating pain, that causes us to seek out companions to help carry the burden.

Mistaken identity: n.:
the cops didn't do their homework: penalize the victim.

Misunderstanding: n.:
the mother of Conflict.

Mixed message: n.:
a very common source of confusion.
We air commercials telling kids that drugs will do them harm—during programs sponsored by companies that market pain killers, antacids, sleeping pills. Our leaders tell us that anyone who breaks the law must be severely punished, then freely pardon each other for flouting the highest laws of the land. We preach the importance of sobriety, but most of the programming that the targets of the preaching watch is sponsored by beer companies. The government funds intrusive measures against tobacco use and spends as much per year artificially maintaining the market price of tobacco.

Mob: n.:
a group of people gathered for the purpose of practicing non-constitutional democracy.
The effective intelligence and self control of a mob are inversely proportional to the number involved.

Model: v.t.:
to construct a condensed and simplified depiction of an interesting phenomenon, which, while it will not act like the original, will be prettier to look at.
  n.:
1) an individual chosen to represent a portion of the populace, but be prettier to look at.
2) a depiction of things the way we think they should be.

Moderation: n.:
abstention; abolition.
Heinlein advocates "To enjoy the flavor of life, take big bites. Moderation is for monks."

Modern: adj.:
having given up or rejected traditional values.

Modest: adj.:
1) inadequate.

2) prudish.

Modesty: n.:
a trait in which those around us are much deficient, compared to ourselves.

Mohel: n.:
hieratic surgeon who takes tips.

Molasses: n.:
derrieres of small, burrowing insectivores.

Monarchy: n.:
rule by one; so long as that one has a really large army to command.

Money: n.:
principal object of worship in all the civilized nations.
the vitamin that empowers good behavior, for as Twain noted, "the lack of money is the root of all evil."

"Money can't buy happiness": myth:
a philosophy espoused primarily by people who want you to give them your money.

Monitoring: gerund:
the euphemistic description of an employer spying on his employees. The current practice, pervasive and invasive, represents the ultimate triumph of the Reagan years: they have privatized Big Brother.

Moral: adj.:
1) pandering to my fears, neuroses and prejudices. Especially applied to sexual matters, so that profiteering would be moral, while a premarital affair would not.

2) furthering my political goals, especially if it can be done outside the public eye.

Moral crisis: n.:
acceptance of any morality other than my own.

Moral high ground: n.:
the vantage held by my side, or, more likely, by the side with the bigger battalions.

Moral suasion: n.:
threats and bribery, dressed up in diplomatic language.

Morale: n.:
a valuable asset, easily spent and exhausted. The difference between a team and a committee.

Morality: n.:
1) if it feels good, don't do it.
2) a set of rules for others to live by.
3) the conviction that those who do not bind their behavior to your standards do not, and should not, have rights.

Morals: n.:
the rules and standards of behavior by which you are to conduct your private life.
Alley cats, wolves and sharks are traditionally unencumbered.

Mortal: adj.:
not God, no matter what the title on the door says.

Mortician: n.:
bier baron.

Mosquito: n.:
an annoying, noisy little bloodsucker without a law degree.

Moth: n.:
butterfly of the evening.

Motherhood: n.:
1) the sacrosanct powder with which the population bomb is loaded.
2) nocturnal lepidoptery.

Mouse: n.:
apprentice rat.

Mouth: n.:
custom foot holder.

Mouth-to-mouth: adv.:
one of a series: meet eye-to-eye; confront nose-to-nose; fight hand-to-hand; negotiate mouth-to-mouth.

Mrs. Grundy: proper name:
arch proponent of the philosophy "no nudes is good nudes."
Reputed to be a personal friend of Jesse Helms.
Believed to have moved from Boston to Peoria sometime in the 60s.

Mud wrestling: n.:
a spectator sport popular because of its similarity to wet T-shirt contests or political campaigning.

Mudslinger: n.:
as the gunslinger was to the range wars of the Old West, the mudslinger is to the campaigns of the New Age.

Mugging: n.:
private-sector equivalent of an IRS hearing.

Mugger: n.:
1) face dancer.
2) dancer on other peoples' faces.

Multinational: adj.:
owning the allegiance of more than one national government.

Muppet: proper name:
the only media icon of the second half of the Twentieth Century that a concientious parent would want their child to emulate.

Murder: v.t.:
to cause a death I disapprove of; to kill without sanction from state or military authority.
n.:
homicide absent the authorization of me, of my social group, of my church, or of some state which I deign to recognize.

Murphy's Law: n.:
"If there are two ways to do something and one of them is wrong, someone will do it the wrong way."
Amazingly, Murphy was not a political commentator.

Museum: n.:
municipal display-case; the center for art and science for the many.

Music: n.:
the language spoken at home by Erato, Calliope, Polymnia and their sisters.

Musical score: n.:
1) purchase at a Grateful Dead concert.
2) see the "Bolero" sequence in the movie "10".

Mutually Assured Deterrence: n.:
a public policy excellently characterized by its acronym.

Myopia: n.:
the inability to see detail beyond the end of one's nose. A common and apt metaphor for the planning ability of business executives, economists and politicians.

Mystery: n.:
a phenomenon whose relationships have not yet advertised themselves to me.

Mythology: n.:
your body of lore in support of religious philosophy, *vs.* my divine revelation, his baseless superstition.

N

NATO: acronym:
   Not Any Too Operable; Now America Takes Over.
   The Parchment Tiger of Europe.
   Godfather to the Treaty of Maastricht.

NIMBY: acronym:
   prime development real estate—optimum siting location for the extra jails called for by anti-crime measures. Also, the best place to site new power plants, landfills, highways necessitated by my consumption habits.

Nader: n.:
   Middle English for a venomous reptile, a snake in the grass.
   It's remarkable how little the meanings of words change over time.
   Modern English for "Son of Ludd."

Naif: n.:
   once a babe in the woods, now a babe in the lobbies and halls of Congress, a much more predatory environment.

Naive: adj.:
   not having the organ of cynicism properly developed.

Naivete: n.:
the foremost character trait of freshman legislators.

Naked: adj.:
undecorated; contrast with nude, which is merely unclothed. Consider, for example, the difference between "naked aggression" and "nude aggression."

Narcissist: n.:
an insufferable egoist who thinks he's prettier than I am.

Narrator: n.:
unseen source of the voice that explains what you're supposed to be seeing in what you're watching.

Narrow-minded: adj.:
unable to encompass and endorse my point of view.

Nation: n.:
an affiliation bounded not by the natural bonds of family or race, but by the unnatural bonds of politics.

National: adj.:
parochial on a grand scale.

National park: n.:
a parcel of public land held away from the harvesters and exploiters, so that the developers and hucksters can get their fair chance.

Nationalism: n.:
"My country, right or wrong…," which only needs to be invoked when it is wrong.

Nationalist: n.:
one with so much religious fervor that it spills over from the pulpit to the podium; one who seeks to evangelize for politics as well as religion.

Natural law: n.:

1) one which does not depend on police for its enforcement or lawyers for its definition.
2) one I believe in.

Natural selection: n.:
the medium which defines "fittest" in "survival of the fittest;" scientific name for "luck."

Nature *vs*. Nurture: myth:
a major philosophical conflict of our time.
Nature: you were born that way; it's all in the genes; it's not your fault.
Nurture: environment means everything; it's all your parents' fault; it's not your fault.
Note that either way, it's not *my* fault, which is the most important consideration.

Navel contemplation: n.:
a difficult form of meditation, requiring one to move one's focus several inches from the center of one's interests.

Naysayer: n.:
one who styles his debating style on the writings of Ross Perot.

Nazi: n.:
short for Nazarene;

1) anyone who seeks to curtail my activities.
2) historical scapegoat for the popularity of anti-Semitism during the first half of the twentieth century.

Necessity: n.:
mother of Invention, daughter of Improvidence. Nobody knows the father.

Negative political ad: n.:
Truth in Advertising, as filtered through the political campaign process.

Neglect: v.t.:
treat with the consideration that conservatives show for any group that does not have its own PAC.

Negligee: n.:
a (nearly) transparent plea for attention.

Negligent: adj.:
having allowed any act or event that inconvenienced me.

Negligible: adj.:
having the importance of the Second Amendment to a liberal Congress, the Fourth to a conservative Congress or the Ninth to any Congress.

Neighbor: n.:
someone who has the good fortune to be able to bask in our reflected glory. Good ones build good fences. Perhaps they just don't want to be blinded by the reflection.

Neighborhood: n.:
the teenager who lives down the block.

Neighborhood Watch: n.:
painless community service for Peeping Toms.

Neo-Nazi: n.:
a walking illustration of Heinlein's maxim that "a generation which ignores history has no past and no future."

Nepotism: n.:
a benevolent institution by which relatives of officeholders are kept off the welfare rolls.

Nerd: n.:
an individual of deficient personality, "half a nebbish, half a turd," who is the one you have to go to to get your computer working. A notoriously vengeful breed.

Nest egg: n.:
something of value, set aside in anticipation of its future maturity; routinely converted by inflation into a goose egg.

Neurotic: n.:
normal.

Never: adv.:
when campaign promises are kept, commercials are honest and taxes are lowered.

"Never again": slogan:
It's my turn.

New age: adj.:
describing a movement characterized by the fact that its followers act as though they were born yesterday. You can't get a much newer age than that.

New age music: n.:
mood music for those who subscribe to Stout's *Anglo-Saxon Theory of Emotions and Dessert*: freeze them and hide them in the belly.

New Deal: n.:
another go around with the same old stacked deck.

New Frontier: n.:
the border probed when acquisitiveness and aggression are turned inward.

New World Order: n.:
Bush League of Nations.

News: n.:
propaganda, gossip, and editorial bias masquerading as reportage. On TV, the programming element used to demarcate the boundaries of prime time.

News leak: n.:
a press release they need to be able to deny.

Newspaper: n.:
local source for coupons, sale announcements, want ads, legal announcements, the comics and yesterday's TV news. Noted for its utility in wrapping fish or old coffee grounds, or for lining the cages of birds.

Newspeak: n.:
the language used by the press. Orwell was much too optimistic and conservative in his estimates of how badly the press could redefine the public vocabulary.

Newt: n.:
a salamander wannabe: a slimy little mud puppy that's not evolved enough to qualify as the lizard it tries to look like.

Webster's gives an alternate definition as "EFT", which is the acronym for Electronic Funds Transfer. Life imitates art?

The benevolent and beneficial nature of the Newt's relationship to Mankind has been known at least since the time of Macbeth.

Newter: v.t.:
homophonious description of the Speaker's intentions for the Government.

Newton's 3rd Law of Politics: adage:
for every action, there is a reactionary

Newtralize: v.t.:
restructure Government so as to weaken those elements which empower the individual over the corporate entity, while strengthening those that work the opposite way.

Nicotine addiction: n.:
a deplorable condition leading to aberrant behavior, especially when manifested in Congressional campaign funds.

Nigger: n.:
the title of a book by Dick Gregory.

Night: n.:
time of sufficiency, as: "Once a king, always a king, but once a night is enough", which is heresy to a man in his 20s, pessimism to one in his 30s, boasting in his 40s, wishful thinking in his 50s, nostalgia in his 60s.

Nimby: n (from acronym):
The nymph of the Banana.

"No": expletive:
"'No' always means 'No.'" By symmetry, "Yes" never means "Yes." Welcome to the Wonderful World of Political Correctness.

"No Comment": phrase:
"I don't want to get into a pissing contest with someone who has the press in his corner."

No moss: n. phrase:

1) money, sex, drugs and rock and roll—what the Rolling Stones gather.

2) a delicate produce harvested from little Hands of Stone.

"No pain, no gain": motto:
a philosophy espoused by manufacturers of pain relievers. "Mortification of the flesh benefits the soul" updated to a sound bite.

Nobility: n.:
a character trait that occasionally allows one to act like a hero of historical fiction.

Noble gas: n.:
historically, a perennial source of amusement and topic of discussion among the aristocracy. See Twain's *1601, or Fireside Conversation As It Was In the Time of the Tudors*.

Noble metal: n.:
the metals used as money or symbols of wealth. So called because of the propensity of the nobility to acquire them, no matter what the price to the populace.

Noble savage: myth:
an artifact of the human desire for balance and symmetry: if the nobility are so savage, then the savages must be noble.

Nominalize: v.t.:
freeze in time; to take a process and declare it as a thing.

Nominally: adv.:
in your dreams.

Non culpabilis: **phrase:**
lawyerese for "I am not a crook."

Noncombatant: n.:
a participant in a war whose job description does not involve using a weapon, except staff officers, who are considered to be honorary combatants.
Before the advent of long-range artillery and aerial bombardment, noncombatatants were at reduced risk of attack in wars. Now, it is a distinction without a difference.

Nondemoninational: adj.:
in the manner of my religion, but without naming my Deity directly. Used primarily in reference to government-sponsored prayer.

None of the above: phrase:
a shoo-in in any election he chooses to run in.

Nonfeasance: n.:
[criminal] failure to perform legally required functions.
So universally experienced in bureaucracies that it is no longer prosecuted.
The only saving grace of many elected officials.

Nonhuman: n.:
pagan; heathen; *goy; untermensch*; gentile; civilian; enemy; alien; anyone who does not belong to a group approved of by me.

Nonpartisan: adj.:
1) describing my side's magnanimous position.
2) of an election, one where the political parties don't have to admit which candidates they're appointing.

Normal: adj.:
in science, standing straight up and sticking out; out of science, lying down and blending in.

Nose: n.:
an organ at home in many places, especially in the air and in other peoples' business.

Nostalgia: n.:
exudation of a defective memory; the past, seen through rose-colored glasses.
Nostalgia is proof positive that hindsight is not always 20-20.

Nota bene: motto:
portmanteau term including NOTA, acronym for None Of The Above, plus bene, Latin for good. A popular sentiment in election years.

Nothing: n.:
sacred entity to the Me generation.

"Nothing is worth dying for": mantra:
1) "Nothing is worth my dying for;" the rest of you are a different story.
2) "Nothing is worth killing for;" the pacifist philosophy that only survives when guaranteed by those who don't subscribe to it.
3) "Nothing is worth living for;" the world view of those with a justly deserved inferiority fixation.

Nouvelle: adj.:
French for "undersized and overpriced."

NRA: initials:
Nazi Republican Army, to the anti-gun lobby.

Nuclear family: n.:
parent(s) and child(ren) isolated from all others. The "traditional family unit" of the nuclear age, so called because it's the right size of group to fit into a bomb shelter.

Nude: adj.:
attired in the garb designed by the Creator; therefore, blasphemous in the eyes of the religious.

Nudism: n.:
appreciation of the Creator's taste in design; sinful and sacreligious. "If the Good Lord had meant for Man to be a nudist, we'd be born without clothes."

Number one priority: n.:
a problem common to Old White Men.

Nuremberg defense: n.:
a legal ploy that was invalidated in the American legal system from the Truman administration until the Nixon administration. The validation was repeated during the Reagan administration.
"I was only following orders."

Nut: n.:
1) old slang for "head", the traditional seat of intelligence;
2) slang for someone whose reason has left him (or her);
3) slang for the male gonad, which the feminists attribute as the seat of male intelligence.

Nuts: expletive:
appropriate response to a demand for surrender from the commander of an overwhelming force.

Nymphomaniac: n.:
a woman whose sexual appetites are greater than mine.

O

O: proper name:
  storied French lady.

OPEC: acronym:
  Organization of Petroleum Extorting Countries.

Obedience: n.:
  what we demonstrate to authority—when they're watching.

Obesity: n.:
  disease caused by overactive fork.

Objective reporting: n.:
  telling my side of the story.

Objectivity: n.:
  the enviable ability to reach agreement with my opinions.

Obscenity: n.:
  lewdness. Who was it that said "I may not be able to define obscenity, but I know what I like"?

Obscure: v.t.:
  render unclear or difficult to recognize or understand; "clarify" in lawyerese.

Obscurity: n.:
the kind of fame allotted to Vice Presidents, majority whips and offensive linemen.

Obsequious: n.:
showing the style of independence and confrontational form appropriate to a suitor, or an employee.

Observatory: n.:
a place for authorized peering into the private lives of stars.

Obstetrician: n.:
Doctor Stork.
As a predictable result of the activities of the legal profession, this species is becoming endangered in the United States.

Obviously: adv.:
apparently.

Occupation: n.:
an activity that takes possession of your life.

Oedipus: proper name:
a young fellow who loved his mother, not wisely but too well.

Offal: n.:
the awful parts of the animal, that you'd never want to eat. Used in the production of sausage.

Offend: v.t.:
1) describe too accurately for comfort.
2) mention something I'm not mature enough to deal with.

Offensive: adj.:
a little too close to home.

Office automation: n.:
car phone, car fax, laptop computer.

-oid: adj. suffix:
shaped like; imitating. As "factoid: imitation of a fact", "spheroid: shaped like a ball", etc.

Oil: n.:
Nectar of the Gods of Industry.
v.t.:
lubricate; ease the operation of. An mechanical term; the political equivalent would be "bribe" or "contribute to."

Old: adj.:
once, honored, valued; now, obsolete, due to be discarded, used up.

Old Age: n.:
a stage of life so unpleasant and unrewarding that the Politically Correct feel a need to dress it up in glowing euphemisms. We typically only get through it by considering the alternative.

Old South: proper name:
the era and area of American history where bed linens were sold in "44 Stout" or "6-3/8," rather than "twin" or "full." The favored size was "wizard" instead of "king."

Omnipotent: adj.:
a meaningless sound much favored by the devout, who rarely understand potent, much less omni-.

Omnipresent: adj.:
sharing the nature of the Government as it applies to your private life.

Oncogeny: n.:
oncogeny decapitates phylogeny.

One: adj.:
enough hands on a scientist, in the eyes of Congressional committees. "What we need here is some one-handed scientists and no more of this 'on the other hand' stuff."

One-armed bandit: n.:
to liberals, the former majority leader of the Senate.

Opera: n.:
histrionic musical spectacle, where most of the audience have gone to be seen.

Opiate: n.:
number of minds. According to Marx, religion was the opiate of the masses. Marx lived before the advent of daytime television.

Optimistic: adj.:
having the belief that this is the best of all possible worlds. cf. PESSIMISTIC.

Oral contraception: n.:
a method of birth control that has been around since a long time before anyone invented Pills, or even pills. According to some accounts, lipstick was invented to advertise it.

Orbit: v.i.:
to fall forward in such a clever way that you keep ending up where you started.

Orbital mechanics: n.:
1) NASA's shuttle-flying repair crews.
2) one of those nasty scientific fields where things don't work right: in order to speed up you have to slow down and in order to slow down you have to speed up.

Orc: n.:
a creature from J R R Tolkien's fantasy world, having the personality of a tax collector.

Orchestra: n.:
the traditonally objectionable sax and violins on television.

Orchid: n.:
paradoxical flower that is named like the male's sex organs, but looks like the female's.

Orgasm: n.:
an activity rediscovered by the unnamed prior generation to the Boomers, who raised it to an object of adulation.

Orgasmic: adj.:
simulated.

Original sin: n.:
a very difficult accomplishment in modern times, but a popular goal, nonetheless.

Orthodox: adj.:
in religion, acting on the conviction that the appropriate way to advocate their beliefs is at the point of a bayonet;
in medicine, working to the doctrine "if you can't cut it out, drug it into submission."

Outrageous: adj.:
ostentatiously not in accordance with my whims and preferences.

Outsource: v.i.:
a way for management to declare that they think that someone else can manage important parts of their business better than they can.

Over the counter: adj.:
set up to hide the under-the-table.

Overawed: adj.:
responding to the presence of the overly odd.

Overdose: n.:
more than the system can tolerate. Lenny Bruce died of an overdose of police; Jean Seberg died of an overdose of FBI.

Overheated economy: n.:
one that has had too much paper thrown on it just as it was starting to cook.

Overindulgence: n.:
exercise of appetites beyond what I would be willing to admit to.

Overreaction: n.:
standard response to being forced to acknowledge a problem.

Oversexed: adj.:
wanting it more often than I do.

Oversight committee: n.:
a body empanelled for the purpose of overlooking violations by affiliates of the side of the majority and looking over actions by the members of the party of the minority.

Oversleep: n.:
an oxymoron: there is no such thing as too much sleep.

Overtake: v.i.:
follow the philosophy of taxing agencies.

Overtax: v.t.:
perform an impossible act, according to the belief system of liberal governments.

Ovine: adj.:
demonstrating the acute critical faculties and leadership qualities of a party stalwart.

Owl: n.:
traditional animal archetype for intelligence. Characteristic traits include an inquisitive vocabulary, nocturnal habits, and a carnivorous diet. They also bathe and preen less often than other birds. Few are noted for their melodious voices.

Ox: n.:
gorer of farmers, goree of causes; traditional measure of quickness or strength.

Oxford: proper name:
famous British university, home of another fine dictionary, recently recruited as a field for promoting American celebrity books.

oxymoron: n.:
a phrase that contradicts itself or names something that cannot exist. Examples include "Ethics in Government Act", "Truth in Advertising", "Generally Accepted Accounting Principles."
Traditional forms include "military intelligence," "marijuana initiative," "liberal arts education."

Oyster: n.:
bivalve mollusc noted for its taciturn nature and its habit of concealing pearls; considered edible in some circles.
Swift notes "He was a bold man that first eat an oyster." Given the appearance of the the oyster when out of the shell, that man was probably French.

Ozone: n.:
hyperactive oxygen: a chemical compound we have to prevent in the air near the ground and preserve in the air near space; its presence in the former damages the lungs and its absence from the latter damages the skin.
A couple of generations ago, it was the prototype of pure air and people with lung ailments were sent to natural sources to improve their health.

P

PAC: n.:
either a boot or a political pressure group.
With continued use, they tend to develop similarly attractive odors. The Supreme Court has declared that PACs have the same constitutional rights as citizens. No one has dared to suggest that PACs might also have similar responsibilities to private citizens.

Pablum: n.:
the meat of mass entertainment.

Pacifism: n.:
a philosophy that can only endure under the protection of a government with a strong military.

Pad: v.t.:
write down; as pad an expense account.

Paid political announcement: n.:
Lullaby of Broadcast.

Pain: n.:
the gauge we use to determine that we are still alive.

Pale: adj.:
lacking in color; white. Hence, *outside the pale* for being beyond the protection of the law.

Pan: proper name:
the original "old goat."
  v.t.:
describe in the same glowing terms used by theater critics to describe any production they can't understand.

Panhandle: v.i.:
reach out and put the touch on someone.

Panic: v.i.:
"When in trouble, or in doubt, run in circles, scream and shout." The state of mind experienced by bureaucrats when faced by anything unexpected.

Parable: n.:
a lie in fable's clothing.

Paradigm: n.:
dogma.

Paradox: n.:
a buzzword used to disguise my inability to see the relationship between two things.

Paragon: n.:
larger-than-life figure, usually with the feet of clay covered and hidden.

Paramilitary: adj.:
adapting military training and tactics, but not military justice or restraint.

Paramilitary organization: n.:
an army no nation will claim.

Paranoia: n.:
a condition induced by close observation of the activities of government.
Just because you're paranoid doesn't mean they're not out to get you. Survivorship for the 90s.

Parasite: n.:
a creature bearing the same relationship to its host as a lawyer to his client.

Parasitism: n.:
the ecological relation of a government to its populace, or of the human race to the rest of the biosphere.

Parent: n.:
one who has chosen to shirk the responsibilities of raising children.

Pari-mutuel: n.:
gallop poll.

Parkinson's disease: n.:
[bureaucracy] Parkinson's law.

Parkinson's Law: n.:
the staff expands to exceed the budget; the accomplishments do not expand.

Parliament: n.:
the inspiration for the story of the Tower of Babel.

Parliamentary Procedure: n.:
a body of rules compiled from observation of the activities of unsupervised playtime at kindergarten and of the feeding frenzies of sharks.

Parole: n.:
half-time in the going-to-prison game.

Partisan: adj.:
  your side's selfish position.
    n.:
  Soldier without a barracks.
  If against the left, a freedom fighter; if against the right, a communist insurrectionist; if against me, a terrorist.

Party discipline: n.:
  lampshades will not be worn as hats, clothing will remain decent in the main room, and no one except the entertainment committee is allowed to spike the punchbowl.

Party of the first part: n.:
  baby's first haircut.

Passive restraint: n.:
  the product of the consumer advocates' conclusion that the average driver is an ineducable dolt; enshrined in law by a Congress that has the same belief.

Passover: n.:
  the holy day on which the Jews celebrate the death of a generation of Egyptian firstborn children.

Pastoral: adj.:
  pertaining to either preachers or pastures. The point of commonality seems to be between the contents of sermons and the ordinary contaminants of pastures.

Paternalistic: adj.:
  maternalistic.

Patient: n.:
  client of a physician. So named in recognition of the personality trait most required in dealing with physician's appointment schedules. Have you ever noticed that they deliberately call it a "waiting room?"

Patriot: n.:
newspeak for traitor.

Patriotism: n.:
first refuge of a member of a Republican administration.

Patron: n.:
one who has at least paid for the right to be patronizing.

Pawn: n.:
the crucial player in the conflicts between occupants of the seats of power: pawns are the cannon fodder of symbolic wars.
v.t.:
sell an article, frequently not of one's ownership, for a drastically reduced price, on the pretext that it is merely security for a short loan and will soon be redeemed.

Peace: n.:
that stage of war that is prosecuted by diplomats and merchants rather than by soldiers.

Peaceful protest: n.:
1) one where no one is killed, if for my cause;

   one where no one shows up, if against me.

2) one that will be safely ignored, except by the news media, which was the whole idea in the first place.

A peaceful protest generally provides air time only for leaders and spokespersons, and is therefore the preferred kind.

Peacock: n.:
bird that dresses like a drag queen.

Pearls before swine: phrase:
practical priority for evacuating a burning house.

Peccadillo: n.:
a minor or conventional sin, especially of the kind that elicits a "nudge, nudge, wink, wink" reaction from nonparticipants.

Peckerwood: n.:
obsolete spelling of Packwood.

Pecs: n.:
body-building slang for the muscles that give a weight lifter a bigger bust than his girl friend.

Pederast: n.:
unabbreviated spelling of "priest."

Pedophilia: n.:
love of children.

Peeping Tom: proper name:
president of the Coventry branch of the Godiva fan club.

Peeping tom: n.:
dream date for a female exhibitionist.

Peignoir: n.:
a loose woman's morning dress.

Pejorate: v.t.:
to make a speech about the other side's position.

Pejorative: adj.:
having the property of making things worse.

Pell-mell: adv.:
as highly structured and organized as the final two weeks of a congressional session.

Penicillin: n.:
medical marvel and wonder drug of the '50s, cattle feed of the '70s, public health menace of the '90s. A full career by anyone's standards.

Penile: adj.:
pertaining to a system of punishment and oppression, according to feminists.

Penile dementia: n.:
the ultimate outcome of too much playing of "mine is bigger than yours."

Penis envy: n.:
the emotion that motivates Viagra sales.

Penitent: adj.:
showing the proper response for having hurt my feelings.

Penitentiary: n.:
seminary of incarceration. A place to regret having been caught.

Pentagon papers: n.:
computer printouts that cost $374 per ream.

Penury: n.:
the natural state of the governed.

Peon: n.:
underling. So named from the treatment he can expect from his employer.

People: v.t.:
populate a region by exterminating or enslaving the natives and replacing them with your own folk.

Peppery: adj.:
pushy, loud and obnoxious.

Per cent: n.:
an arithmetic concept that we all supposedly learned in grade school, heavily misused by pseudoscientists because everyone thinks they understand it and it sounds mathematical.
For example:

give 110%: work fairly hard.
> There is only 100% (all) to give: Pheidippides gave 100% at Marathon, and he didn't live to tell of it.
> The common usage of the phrase is a clear indication of the level of numeracy of athletes and the "journalists" who adulate them.

400% less than: 25% (or 20%) of.

200% more than: 200% of; twice.

Perfect: adj.:
the way I like it.
> v.t.:

improve marginally, as a product or process.

Perfidy: n.:
criticism, by a friend.

Performance: n.:
ability to accomplish.

Performance art: n.:
self-indulgence of the attention-starved.
If, as Bayans holds, minimalism is the Anorexia of the "fine arts," then surely performance art is its Bulimia.

Perjury: n.:
sworn testimony by an Administration official.

Perpetual motion machine: n.:
a bit of technological mythology, embodied in the Energizer bunny, probably inspired by observation of the oral action of politicians.

Persecution: n.:
the price of being different.
Persecution is the action of a mob, acting jointly or severally, or of a power bloc not reasonably distinguishable from a mob.

Person: n.:
a human of unspecified gender; not to be confused with a human of indeterminate gender, who is not to be considered a person under a conservative administration.

Personal: adj.:
my business, and none of yours.

Personality: n.:
a character that women attribute to girls they don't think are good looking.

Personification: n.:
pasting the attributes of humans onto animals and inanimate objects; the *lingua franca* of the Disney studios.

Perspective: n.:
something that is not taught by a church that teaches that both masturbation and murder are mortal sins, equal in the eyes of the church and of God.

Perverse: adj.:
impishly committed to being in the wrong.

Pervert: n.:
a scoundrel who has the nerve to do things I only dare to read about.

Perverted: adj.:
sexually creative.
Kinky is stimulating your lover with a feather; perverted is using the whole chicken.

Pessimistic: adj.:
having the belief that this is the best of all possible worlds. cf. OPTIMISTIC.

Pet: n.:
head-of-household child surrogate.

Pet rock: n.:
cultural icon of the 70s, celebrating the vivacity and initiative of the career bureaucrat.

Petard: n.:
French for bootstrap; that which you are hoist by your own.

Phallic: adj.:
the shape of things to come.

Phallus: n.:
the staff of life, especially to adolescents.

Phallusy: n.:
feminist myth; the falsity that has launched a thousand polemics.

Philanderer: n.:
a benefactor who loves his fellow persons.

Philanthropic: adj.:
gay.

Philanthropy: n.:
the cream of human kindness.

Philistine: n.:
one whose esthetic values are different from mine.

Philosophy: n.:
love of sophistry; addiction to the adventure of exploring the reaches of ones own mind.

Phlebotomist: n.:
bipedal medicinal leech.

Phone: n.:
nickname for the modern Slavemaster.

Phony: adj.:
demostrating the veracity, integrity and truthfulness of my opponent.

Phylism: n.:
the belief that one phylum, usually animals, is more worthy of protection and consideration than the others.

Physics: n.:
1) the study of the interactions of matter and energy; a practitioner is called a physicist.
2) a family of medicines used to clear the alimentary tract; the prescriber is called a physician.

The similarity in names is probably due to the fact that the Physics class in school is about as popular as a dose of salts.

Pick of the litter: n. phrase:
bag lady's lunch.

Pickup: n.:
the natural leader among the species *Automobile*.
This can be seen by the lines of lesser automobiles to be found behind them on the highways.
Many pickups seem to have been subjected to a medical procedure that left them surgically attached to the left lane.

"A picture is worth a thousand words": aphorism:
prophetic prediction of the bandwidth problems of the Internet.

Piety: n.:
the state of living as though confounded by the belief that one's All-knowing All-seeing God cannot know the content of one's heart, unless that heart is worn openly and ostentatiously on the sleeve.

Pinch runner: n.:
lady's souvenir of her trip to Rome or Athens.

Pious: adj.:
professing devotion to God. Usually, professing devotion greater than yours.

Pissant: n.:
a small ant found around latrines used by diabetics.

Pissing contest: n.:
negative political campaign. The idea is to see which candidate can have the greater impact on the electorate.

Pit stop: n.:
an event in auto racing where a team can service a race car in about the same amount of time it takes a candidate to change his position on the issues.

Plagiarism: n.:
lazy research.
To copy from one is considered plagiarism; to copy from many is considered research.

Plagiarize: v.i.:
enjoy the butter without having had to work the churn.

Plague: n.:
any serious disease that lends itself to being blamed on the victims.

Planned obsolescence: n.:
the twenty-second amendment.

Plastic surgery: n.:
cosmetic medical procedures intended to make the recipient look as though made of plastic.

Playing God: v. phrase:
taking an action or making a decision of which I disapprove, especially in regard to the survival, well-being or wealth of someone of whom I approve.
It is noteworthy that the term is used only in the pejorative and primarily to refer to actions (or inactions) which result in death or loss. Those who preach that God is Love and that God gives life never use the term to refer to, for example, heroic life-prolonging measures.

Pleasure: n.:
gratification.

Pledge of Allegiance: n.:
allegation of loyalty.

Plug and Play: phrase:
computer industry misspelling; properly, "Plug in and Pray."

Plural: adj.:
consisting of one or more, e.g., die/dice, data, media, deer, fish.
For some reason, Americans seem unable to deal with plurals that are formed other than by the addition of-s at the end of the word, using plurals as singular, or, as in the case of die/dice, interchangeably. This problem is primarily of interest to anal retentives.

Plutocrat: n.:
successful capitalist.

Poetry: n.:
a literary form intended to appeal to emotion rather than to intelligence. This is called making a virtue of necessity.

Poland: proper name:
a nation saddled with a stereotyped image of rampant moronity. Not to be confused with Poll-land, the Columbian home of professional morons.

Polemics: n.:
the language of American common law, and the politics that American common lawyers go in for.

Police brutality: n.:
"They arrested me!"

Political asylum: n.:
legislature. Tragically, the inmates are in charge of this one.

Political bazaar: n.:
metaphorical marketplace of the politically bizarre; where you go to buy politicians.

Political capital: n.:
slush fund.

Political conscience: n.:
what a legislator votes in accordance with, *i.e.*, the commands of his campaign contibutors.

Political contribution: n.:
lease payment.

Political correctness: n.:
a modern aberration which imposes on the productive the neuroses and phobias of those who are not.

Political party: n.:
how your congressman spends his leftover campaign funds.

Political science: n.:
the only kind that gets time on the Evening News.

Politically correct: n.:
intellectually incorrect.
Political correctness is the Left's attempt to abuse power through censorship in response to the Right's obscenity laws.

Polling place: n.:
locale of voting, named after the practice of removing the horns from cattle to make them more tractable.

Pollution: n.:
That index by which an industrial nation measures its superiority over simpler, lesser societies.

Pollyanna: proper name:
the President's principal speechwriter.

Polygamy: n.:
polygyny. Any of the forms where there are multiple husbands are unmentionable in American English.

Polymorphously perverse: adj.:
Freud's sesquipedalian way of affirming the folk wisdom that "opposites attract" and "like draws to like", both at once.

Pompous: adj.:
having the public manner of a campaigning politician, televangelist or boxing promoter.

Poor: *adj*:
1) not very good.
2) not very wealthy.

Popular: adj.:
1) vapid; insipid.
2) cheap.

Pork barrel: n.:
favored dining locale of the well-connected.

Pornography: n.:
how-to manuals for the sexually repressed. Or, how-not-to manuals, for the really repressed.

Portentous: adj.:
pretentious.

Posthaste: adv.:
a modern single-word oxymoron.

Postal: adj.:
pertaining to the mails, as US Postal Service. From the latin for "after" or "later than."

Pot: n.:
1) defining element of a chamber, in conjunction with a window.
2) a substance that is bad for your health, in that it will get your body thrown into jail.

Pot of Gold: n.:
a traditional phrase recognizing the street value of sensamilla, charas, or even reasonable ganja.

Potential: n.:
unrealized possibility; generally cast as a burden of expectation.

Poverty: n.:
the natural condition of the governed.

Power: n.:
1) the capacity, as opposed to the ability, to apply suasion and exercise control.
2) the ultimate aphrodisiac.

   At the highest levels, it seems to manifest in two contrasting styles: those who exercise one at a time, as the tabloid version of Jack Kennedy, and those who go for us wholesale, like Richard Nixon.
3) force, especially armed force.

Power-hungry: adj.:
prepared to run for office. Or for God, if you can afford the air time.

Power-mad: adj.:
aspiring to a latenight talkshow slot.

Power of attorney: n.:
a formal and legal license to steal.

Power of the purse: n.:
whoever holds the purse gets to wield the power. A method used by Congress to get around the Constitution.

Practical: adj.:
   against Company Policy.

Prayer: n.:
   request for divine intervention.
   Interestingly, these are most commonly formed in the imperative.

Preacher: n.:
   one whose profession is "do as I say, not as I do."

Predator: n.:
   an animal that makes its living by killing: *e.g.*, the wolf, the hawk, the shark, the tiger.
   What boardroom parasites prefer to call themselves.

Pregnancy: n.:
   1) a disease. Contraceptives were formerly sold "for prevention of disease only."
   2) to the right, the punishment for having tasted the pleasures of sex. Any effort that might forestall the punishment must be opposed, with violence if necessary.
   "Think of is as being grounded for 18 years."

Prejudice: n.:
   having the answer before you understand the question.

Prejudiced: adj.:
   espousing an opinion contrary to my own.

Premature: adj.:
   in advance of my schedule; earlier than I wanted.

Premium: n.:
   bribe.
             adj.:
   of superior quality.

Preppie: n.:
member of the what's-in-it-for Me generation.

Prescriptivist: n.:
one who believes that natural law is something decreed, dictated or negotiated to control the behavior of people or things. Typically a lawyer, politician, theologian or social scientist.
Contrast DESCRIPTIVIST.

President: n.:
American English for "king."

Press: n.:
an agency that fervently believes in the constitutional prohibition on abridging freedom of the press, alone of the Bill of Rights.

Pressure group: n.:
an advocacy group aligned with a cause that I don't support.

Prevaricate: n.:
make a public statement.

Preventive detention: n.:
in a democracy, everyone is assumed innocent until arrested.

Priapism: n.:
a medical condition which proves that you can get too much of a good thing.

Price: n.:
an economic property of an item or service that is tenuously related to its value. The difference is highlighted in an observation by Wilde: "What is a cynic? A man who knows the price of everything, and the value of nothing."

Priest: n.:
Roman for pedophile.

Primary: adj.:
   most significant or important, except in regard to elections.
      n.:
   an election so characterized because most of the candidates act like fugitives from grade school.

Primary colors: *nou*n phrase:
   green, carefully camouflaged by Red, White and Blue.

Primate: n.:
   ecclesiastical governor, especially in a tax-supported church. Customarily found in the posture of denying that he is a primate.

Prime rate: n.:
   house odds on the economy.

Prime rib: n.:
   a vegan's idea of Hell; the carnivore's vision of Heaven.

Prime time: n.:
   the hours most valuable to TV programmers: the slow hours after dinner when the family avidly attend the tube to avoid having to listen to each other.

Primitive: adj.:
   deficient in the civilized amenities, such as freeways, airports, industrial pollution, government databases, telephone solicitors, lawyers…

Prince: n.:
   disenchanted frog.

Principal: n.:
   what a politician cultivates in lieu of an ethically superior commodity of similar pronunciation.

Principle: n.:
   template for the application of conscience; the foundation on which morality or ethicality must be built if they are to endure.

Principle traditionally draws much less interest than principal.

Prior restraint: n.:
censorship by intimidation, rather than by accountable action; the prig's fondest dream, as it is of the tyrant.

Prison: n.:
1) Institute of Advanced Study for felons.
2) a place where homosexuals are punished by being held in close and intimate proximity to large numbers of the same sex.
3) a secular monastery where membership is not voluntary.
4) government subsidized housing for political dissidents.

Prison term: n.:
the interval between conviction and parole. For most crimes except drug possession, this will be slightly shorter than the interval between arrest and conviction.

Privacy: n.:
in imposition designed to interfere with the rights of the state and of business to know everything they want to about you.

Private: adj.:
restricted from inspection without the owner's permission, except by government and the police.

Private eye: n.:
Peeping Tom for hire.

Privy: n.:
the little house behind the big house, covering a hole in the ground topped by one or more holes in a board. About a hundred feet back, which would be about a hundred feet too near in the summer and about a hundred feet too far in the winter. Preferably located downwind.

Privy council: n.:
   the Presidential Cabinet. So named in honor of the delicate aroma attendant on the results of their proceedings.

Pro bono: phrase:
   for the good of the appearance.

Pro-life: adj.:
   anti-sex; anti-liberty; pro-military; pro-death penalty. They are pro-pursuit-of-happiness only so long as the method of pursuit meets with their personal approval.

Probate: n.:
   an evil that men do that lives on after them. Where there's a will, there's ill will.

Probation: n.:
   the minor-leagues of criminal sentencing.

Probe: v.t.:
   stick the nose into.

Problem: n.:
   opportunity in disguise. Sometimes the disguise is too good to see through.

PRoblem: n.:
   a situation that can be bent by the media to fit their image of impending catastrophe.

Problematical: n.:
   too complex for one of my glib answers.

Process server: n.:
   a bottom feeder in the attorney pool.

Processor: n.:
   mangler; scrambler; as word processor, data processor, food processor.

Procrastinate: v.i.:
participate in Mankind's oldest and best developed sport.

Procrastination: n.:
optimistic application of the Ostrich Principle: maybe, if I ignore it, it will go away.

Procreation: n.:
the principal hazard of mankind's oldest recreation.

Proctologist: n.:
medical professional whose job description is much the same as that of the Washington bureau chief for a news service: he spends his day looking up assholes.

Proctor: n.:
collegian in charge of enforcing rules; from the same root as proctologist.

Professional: n.:

1) one who pursues an activity for the money, as opposed to an amateur, who does it for the the love of it.

2) a doctor, lawyer, accountant or priest.

Profanity: n.:
the *lingua franca* of physical labor.

Profit: n.:

1) the object of greed.

2) fuel for the engine of Industry.

Program: n.:
the set of instructions that tell a computer how not to do what we want it to.

Progress: n.:
the process by which we rise from simple and savage roots to ever greater depths of organization and accomplishment.

Progression: n.:
a sequence with consistently changing quality from one element to the next, as big, better, best.
The progression of age behaviors would be: infantile, puerile, juvenile, adolescent, mature, adult, wise, crotchety, senile.

Progressive tax: n.:
from each according to his ability to pay; a policy that funds services preferentially from those who use them least.

Prohibition: n.:
1) restriction to the wealthy and/or politically well-connected.
2) "The Noble Experiment", so called because it caused much of America to spend most of its time and money getting drunk as a lord.
3) a dictum designed, if not intended, to increase the popularity of its object.
4) the most reliable known way to generate interest in the heart of a child or adolescent.

Projection: n.:
1) an arbitrary number, chosen to be favorable to the chooser's position, offered in prediction of a future event or state. As, revenue projection, for determining how much tax money to spend next year, before that money is collected.
2) in Freudian psychology, the expectation that someone else will act as badly in a situation as you would, given a free hand.

PRolitics: n.:
Herblock's term for government of the sound bite, by the rigged poll, for the spin doctor, which shall not vanish from the evening news.

Promiscuity: n.:
malicious name for popularity.

Promise: *n.* and v.t.:
   lie.

Proof: n.:
   1)   assertion.
   2)   anything in support of my position.
   Modern usage recognizes many different kinds of proof: proof by induction; proof by deduction; proof by preponderance of evidence; proof by press release; proof by assertion; etc.

Proofread: v.i.:
   learn to identify the most potent liquors by examination of their labels.

Propaganda: n.:
   PR presented in support of a cause not on my support list.

Proper: adj.:
   right—usually far right.

Property: n.:
   the object of avarice. It comes primarily in two varieties: real property—dirt and its appurtenances and products—and private property—the ephemeral accumulations of our little lives—which by contrast must needs be somewhat unreal.

Prophecy: n.:
   fortune-telling in its Sunday-go-to-meeting clothes.

Prophet: n.:
   Speaker for God. Pronounced profit, in recognition of the record of most who claim that title.

Propriety: n.:
   behavior that does not offend me.

Proselytizer: n.:
   walking illustration of the principle "if they could do it, they wouldn't have to talk about it all the time."

Prosperity: n.:
the natural state of the governing class; a land "just around the corner."

Prostate: n.:
a gland that women are blessed by not having.

Prostitution: n.:
commercialized intercourse; short-term rental of sexual services, as contrasted with the longer-term lease represented by marriage.
The oldest commercial method to make ends meet.

Protected wetland: n.:
under a Democratic administration, any place that has ever held a puddle long enough to serve as a birdbath or attract a frog;
under a Republican administration, any land with permanent standing water that has soil properties such as to make it overly expensive to develop.

Protectionism: n.:
trade regulation that benefits someone elses business.

Protest: v.i.:
what the lady does too much, methinks.
This sentiment is shared by Shakespeare in the 17th century and the right in the 20th. Of course, we don't call them ladies any more—they're wo-persons.

Protest group: n.:
an organization formed for the purpose of getting its leadership exposure on television.

Proud: adj.:
swollen with self congratulation.

Providence: proper name:
upscale name for one's guardian angel; affected title for Chance.

Provocative: adj.:
appealing to those desires of mine which I would prefer to deny.

Prudence: n.:
wisdom to the timid.

Prudent: adj.:
acting in a way that would denote cowardice in my enemies.

Prudery: n.:
the worst kind of avarice: that directed toward the theft of another's self respect.

Prudish: adj.:
even more inhibited than I.

Prurient: adj.:
desirable.

Pseudo-science: n.:
a scurrilous compendium of data, observations, anecdotes and conclusions that disagree with my beliefs.

Psychoactive: n.:
1) affecting mood or mind function, *e.g.*, most of the alkaloids, highly sugared foods, hallucinogens, etc.
2) able to attract (mostly) psychotic activists, *pro and contra.*

Psychoanalysis: n.:
the branch of Medicine wherein the patient as well as the doctor embarks on a career in the field.
Based on the teachings of Fraud.

Psychosclerosis: n.:
hardening of the attitudes; a natural disease of age or success; a frequent symptom of wealth.

Pubic: adj.:
not public; private; unsuitable for a 'G' or 'R' rating. The term came into general usage during the Clarence Thomas confirmation hearings.

Public enemy: n.:
high-profile scapegoat for incompetent or corrupt police work.

Public interest: n.:
interests of a powerful pressure group.

Public relations: n.:
after greed, the primary motivation for action by political figures. The basis of advice given to public officials, having supplanted such old-fashioned elements as integrity, concern for the electorate, etc.

Public Television: n.:
TV where you know how much you're actually paying to see the programs.
TV where the commercials come in little spurts before and after the programs, then in practically solid blocks for a couple of weeks at a time four or five times a year.

Pun: n.:
flatus of the body of humor.

Punctuation: n.:
instructions from the writer to the reader, especially the reader-aloud.

Pundit: n.:
media-nese for expert; a commentator whose pronouncements enjoy the same sort of respect as the humor form from which he draws his title.

Punishment: n.:
revenge.

Punk: n.:
  anyone else's teenaged child.

Puppet show: n.:
  a childrens' entertainment intended to educate the young ones about the operation of legislatures and parliaments.

Purist: n.:
  someone who would be an anal-retentive nit picker if he didn't share my interest in the topic in question.

Puritan: n.:
  one who is opposed to sex, lest it lead to dancing.

Purple: adj.:
  traditional color for royalty or prose, which may account for why writers seem to think they deserve to be treated like monarchs. And why everyone in a position of power seems to think they're a writer.

"Put your money where your mouth is": motto:
  see your orthodontist.

Pygalgic: adj.:
  a word (literally, causing a pain in the buttocks) that does not get nearly as much use as it deserves. [pronounced pie-gal-jick]

Pygmy: n.:
  Reader's Digest version of a basketball player.

Pyramid: v.i.:
  to build up from a broad and substantial base to a narrow and inconsequential climax.

Pyromaniac: n.:
  someone who gets his rocks off by getting things hot.

Pyrrhic victory: n.:
  one that ran over budget.

Q

Quail: v.i.:
to shrink in cowardice. Pronounced "quayle".

Quaint: adj.:
Mercantilian adjective for use primarily in tourist-oriented venues; generally translates as "understocked and overpriced."

Quality: n.:
alleged God of Industry, to whom lip service, but little other, is paid.

Qualm: n.:
premonition of conscience.

Quantum: adj.:
a term advertising agents like to use because it sounds scientific and has no conceivable application to their product.

Quarrel: v.i.:
to get along with as with a sibling or a spouse.

Quarterback: n.:
25¢ in change.

Quayle: n.:
Chicken hawk.

Queen: n.:
the most powerful player in the game of chess.
Art imitates life.

Queer: adj.:
liberal+homosexual+activist.

Quest: n.:
a crusade, without the prayer meetings.

Quid pro quo: phrase:
you pad my campaign chest and I'll line your pocket.

Quip: n.:
private citizen's version of a sound bite.

Quis ipsos custodies custodiet: phrase:
"Who shall investigate the special prosecutor?"

Quisling: proper name:
the most famous Norwegian between Leif Ericson and anyone from Lake Wobegon.

Quixotic: n.:
harebrained. Quixotic causes are the only ones routinely worth pursuing.

Quod erat demonstrandum: phrase:
(abbreviated QED) which was to have been demonstrated. Traditional closing line in a proof by assertion, with diversions.

quote: v.t.:
to repeat those portions of the utterance of another that will support my own views.

R

R & B: acronym:
classical music: Rococo and Baroque.

Rabid: adj.:
of animals, showing similar behaviour and characters as a big-city major-league sports fan.

Race: n.:
an attribute that allows us to judge another's worth by a simple inspection of the color of his skin, the shape of his eyes or his face, the clothing he wears. A great time saver, it saves us the necessity of finding out anything about his character, talents or achievements.
Americans base race on skin color: pink,tan, black, yellow and red. Members of other industrial cultures typically have three: my group, those of my skin color, everyone else; some of the non-European cultures will add white, making four. Pre-industrial societies typically have two: us, and everyone else; some will make special provision for the types of the anthropologists they have the most experience with.

Racist: adj.:
white.

Racist: n.:
one who has the misbegotten belief that his race is superior to mine—or the one I'm representing.

Racy: adj.:
bland.
Racy used to mean risque, suggestive or sexy. Anything called racy in its day would be considered dull today.

Radical: n., adj.:
from the latin for "root."
Roots are characteristically contaminated with dirt and fertilizer and require extensive cleaning before becoming useful inside the home.

Radio: n.:
a territory liberated from the liberals for the conservatives by the Nixon administration.

Radioactive waste: n.:
any industrial by-product capable of producing as much radiation exposure as a block of granite or a ski trip.

Raiment: n.:
clothing chosen to advertise our assets and conceal our liabilities of physique. Fortunately, lest we be guilty of false advertising, our taste is usually such as to reverse the effect.

Rain: n.:
the sprinklings from Mother Nature's acid bottle.

Rainbow: n.:
the dreamer's bridge to the other side, where the grass is greener.

Rainbow Coalition: n.:
apparatus used in one man's search for the pot of gold at the end of Pennsylvania Avenue.

Raise the level of awareness: phrase:
  lower the level of tolerance and debar the application of common sense.

Rake: n.:
  short for rakehell: legislator or televangelist.

Rally: n.:
  a gathering for the purpose of listening to "leaders" preach to the converted in such strident tones that the uncommitted can not possibly comprehend the message.

Ralph: proper name:
  the adolescent God of Porcelain, to whom obeisance is regularly made by partiers, bingers and bulimics.

Rampant: adj.:
  extravagant, threatening, and all over the place. The term is used in a favoring sense only in heraldry, where it describes the favorite pose of lions, etc.

Rancid: adj.:
  having an odor reminiscent of a political promise.

Rancor: n.:
  warm blood. When it is said of one that he acted without rancor, it means he acted without anger and without pity.

Random: n.:
  chosen by a system too complex for me to figure out.

Rap: v.t.:
  badmouth.
    v.i.:
  foulmouth.

Rapacity: n.:
  qualifying trait for a seat on the Exchange.

Rape: n.:
the wolf of violence wearing the sheep's clothing of passion.

Rapist: n.:
a would-be music student—one who is looking for someone to teach him to sing soprano in a Heavenly choir.

Rapture: n.:
a mystical event where the body of the true believer is magically transported away from this earth, following the path their wits took long before.

Rat: n.:
a rodent renowned for its similarities to politicians and other career criminals. A rat will eat anything it can reach, foul anything it doesn't eat and gnaw through anything to get to food or escape a trap. Unlike lawyers and politicians, rats can be rewarding pets for those without great wealth and connections; some owners of rats even become emotionally attached to them.

Re-elect: v.t.:
make the same mistake twice.

Reactionary: n., adj.:
having the rational content of a knee-jerk or a sneeze.

Real: adj.:
the way I see it.

Real change: n.:
business as usual, dressed with new rhetoric.

Real estate: n.:
one of the first three, as contrasted with the unreal Fourth (the press) and Fifth (the Arts.)

Real property: n.:
land; as contrasted with unreal property: stocks.

Real world: n.:
 those aspects of daily life that support my position.
 Contrast with ivory tower, inside the beltway, on Wall Street.

Reality: n.:
 my perception.

Reason: n.:
 rationalization; excuse.

Reasonable: adj.:
 conforming to my wishes.

Rebate: n.:
 consumer kickback.

Rebuff: v.t.:
 greet with the same gentile courtesy that a Congressman shows to any supplicant without a PAC.

Rebuttal: n.:
 the "did too" phase of the lawyers' "did not; did too" game.

Recant: v.i.:
 admit that I was right all along.

Recess: n.:
 that block of time scheduled during court proceedings for the attorneys to go out and cavort for the cameras.

Recollection: n.:
 ability to invent. "To the best of my recollection, Senator…"

Record: n.:
 chronicle of misdeeds; as a criminal record, or the record of an officeholder. Some would be tempted to add hit record of a rock-and-roll group to this list.

Recruiter: n.:
 Commercialese for pimp.

Red: adj.:

1) the color people turn on being overstimulated, overheated or embarassed.

2) the color traditionally associated with the Left; the color of fire, blood, anger and danger.

3) extreme red provides heat without light.

Red tape: n.:
the primary product of Government.

Reductio ad absurdum: phrase:

1) a scientific term referring to the logical construction of legal arguments.

2) weight loss infomercial.

Referee: n.:
a beneficiary of Hire the Handicapped programs, whose deficiencies in visual and mental acuity are demonstrated each time he rules for the opposition or fails to rule for our side.

Reflect: v.t.:
lie about. As a mirror reflects your image; literature reflects the culture and morality of its time.

Reform: n.:
an activity highly desirable in others, but unnecessary in ourselves.
v.t.:
eviscerate; as in "we will reform welfare;" "I will reform the city;" etc.

Reformation: n.:
one man's act of faith, taken over by many as their expression of rebellion.

Reformer: n.:
one whose axe is (claimed to be) less bloody than that of the sitting ruler.

Revolutionist without an army. Except in the special case of agrarian reformers, who always seem to have armies.

Regressive tax: n.:
one that funds services preferentially from the people who use them most.

Regulatory reform: n.:
open season on anyone not able to afford their own PAC.

Reinventing Government: phrase:
business as usual, but with new titles on the office doors. Distinguishable from revolution primarily in that in the latter sitting government officials are somewhat more at risk of their lives or their jobs than are the general populace.

Relief: n.:
negative reinforcement.

Relativity: n.:
the scientific principle that pops immediately to mind on entering a legislator's office.

Religion: n.:
a business designed to separate the gullible from their wealth and their autonomy, to the benefit of the leaders of the religion. It operates at the level of faith and rationalization, rather than reason and rationality, tending to the emotional over the intellectual needs of its practitioners. Fortunately, many of the practitioners seem to have no intellectual needs.

Remake: n.:
[movies]

1) an attempt to revive an old script by adding names the modern public knows.
2) an attempt to jumpstart the career of an actor by associating their name with a star of the past.

3) an illustration of the principle that producers, like generals, are always prepared to fight the last war.

Remarkable: adj.:
slightly different from the absolutely ordinary in a way that interests me.

Reminisce: v.i.:
daydream about the good times you wish you'd had when you were younger.

Remora: n.:
a fish that bears the same relationship to a shark as government to industry. The chief difference is in the relative sizes: the remora is considerably smaller than the shark.

Remorse: n.:
the emotion elicited by mornings after.

Render: v.t.:
is it any wonder that we *render* taxes to feed the government and *render* pork carcasses to produce lard, while an actor *renders* the role of Hamlet, and it's all the same word?

Renege: v.i.:
treat an obligation in the same manner as a politician treats campaign promises.

Rent-a-Cop: clause:
a futile pastime: why rent them, when you can go to <major city> and buy them wholesale?

Repartee: n.:
French for "I shoulda said…"

Repent: v.i.:
taste the bitter gall of getting caught.

Repentance: n.:
the goal of punishment. Fortunately, the law accepts the word in lieu of the deed.

Repetition: n.:
1) the active ingredient in most political and many advertising campaigns, based on the principle that if you tell the public something often enough, they will start to believe it regardless of truth.
2) the least intellectual form of humor, after the pratfall.

Reportage: n.:
the fine art of short story composition.
Typically, in the electronic media, continuous coverage is substituted for reportage.

Repression: n.:
a method for amplifying the social and emotional pressures of everyday life until they become explosive.
Sexual repression in America shows in that nearly all our expletives are sexual, in contrast to most of the rest of the world, where scatology dominates. The other contributor to the pattern is the massive public works in water supply and sewage disposal—excrement is no longer associated with illness in the public mind.

Reproductive rights: n.:
the dextrals of paired gonads.
Once upon a time, this term had a broader meaning, but then we experienced a Contract with America.

Republican: n.:
member of a political party sybolized by the elephant—an animal which is huge, gray, and equipped with a nose that it uses to poke into everything around it.

Republican revolution: n.:
the process of combining the Liberal ideal of responsive government, the Centrist ideal of responsible government, and the Conservative ideal of less government to create the modern synthesis: less responsive, less responsible Government.

Reputation: n.:
like an image in the mirror, everyone has one and it's not the one we'd really prefer.

Respect: n.:
a precious commodity that can be obtained only by its expenditure.

Responsibility: n.:
a character trait that other people need to show.

Responsible: adj.:
not my client.

Restore: v.t.:
clean up, modifying to reflect topical tastes in the process.

Retail: n.:
the trade that teaches us why it's no coincidence that the first part of customer is cuss.

Retire: v.i.:
grow a second spare around the middle.

Retirement: n.:
the goal at the end of the long path of toil, which many reach only to discover they can't tolerate the people they've become getting there.

Retrospectroscope: n.:
a device for improving hindsight to 20-20; optics for the Monday morning quarterback (Tuesday morning if he's an ABC fan.)

Revenge: n.:
"justice."

Revenue neutral: adj.:
a plan that takes in approximately as much extra money as the bureaucracy it creates spends.

Reverend: adj.:
honorific extended to those in the clergy. It may be noted that, while many with the title Reverend aspire to the description Right Reverend, none have been known to aspire to be known as Left Reverend.

Review: v.t.:
apply hindsight to, usually with intent to revise.

Revisionist: n.:
an historian, complement of the cynic, who cheerfully (or maliciously, depending on the individual) retells history as he would like for it to have been, rather than the way it was seen to be by the people there at the time.
Hot topics for revisionism have included Hitler's "Final Solution to the Jewish Problem," black Africans' contributions to Western civilisation, the use of the fission bomb in Japan, the actions of the Reagan administration, etc.

Revolting: adj.:
in the fashion of developments, especially housing developments (all made out of ticky-tacky...)

Revolution: n.:
in physics, progression centered about an external axis.
in politics, violent progression from one ruler to the next, generally centered about an external focus of influence.

Rhetoric: n.:
skill in the use of language such that the glamor of the presentation disguises its lack of informative content.

Rhetorical question: n.:
a formal interrogative to which a reply is neither expected nor desired. For example: "Hello; How are you?" "What kind of fool am I?" "Do we really have the best legislature money can buy?"

Rhinoceros: n.:
the only animal whose nose hair is more obtrusive than Al Bundy's.

Rhythm: n.:
1) the universal language in music.

2) a contraceptive method by which Catholics ensure increase in their ranks.

There is a technical term for couples who practice the rhythm method: they're called parents.

Rich: n.:
able to afford personal servants, public servants, and other luxuries; bad for the health: rich foods clog your arteries and upset your digestion; rich employers deflate your compensation; rich lawyers, politicians and industrialists drain your bank account.

Ridiculous: adj.:
having all the respectability and credibility of my opponent's position.

Rigged election: n.:
one where my favored candidate, party or issue did not prevail.

Right: n.:
1) the cause I support—the farther right, the more vocal the support.

2) privilege that has gained an endorsement by either a legislature or a court.

3) a liberty that was granted once upon a time.

Americans seem to have the fixation that if they can get away with something once, when times are good, they are entitled to it as a right forever.

Right-thinking: adj.:
having the belief that you are in the right. Usually, you're merely on the right.

Right of privacy: n.:
a privilege reserved for members of the government and those who own them.

Right to Life: n.:
a movement that advocates capital punishment for doctors who perform abortions and women who get them.

Righteous: n.:
self-righteous.

Rights: n.:
privileges or protections that are left after the rich and powerful preempt the ones they want.

Rights of the poor: n.:
a modern concept which dates to one generation after the introduction of the Raggedy Ann doll.

Rightsize: n.:
fire enough workers to reduce the size of the organization until it's small enough for its managers to handle.

Rigor: n.:
the mathematician's goal of exactitude and completeness. In recognition of the flexibility and creativity this approach engenders, it is named for a biological phenomenon: rigor mortis.

Ringleader: n.:
titular head of an organization; chosen by the real leaders to be the one subject to arrest and detention.

Ripe: adj.:
fully mature, sweet, juicy and ready to reap.
"When a cherry turns red, it's ready for plucking
when a girl turns sixteen, she's ready for
high school."

Rite: n.:
a traditional ceremony made pompous and sententious to disguise the fact that the meaning has been lost in modern times.

Ritual: n.:
a stylized set of actions undertaken to disengage the mind.

Roach motel: n.:
hostelry frequented by attorneys or televangelists. They don't check out because they usually checked in under an assumed name.

Robot: n.:
a mechanical worker highly prized for its inability to form unions or walk off the job when treated the way workers are traditionally treated.

Rock and Roll: n.:
the major motions of an earthquake.

Role model: n.:
someone who poses with pastry (especially cheesecake).

Roll: v.t.:
rob, especially when defenseless; hence the reference to professional athletes as "roll models."

A roll in the hay: phrase:
something better than breakfast in the barn.

Roller coaster: n.:
amusement park attraction inspired by the Dow-Jones average.

Romantic: adj.:
picturesque, fanciful and fictional, as romantic love.

Ronald Reagan: n.:
lead actor in B-movies; promoted to lead player in a B-administration.

Root cause analysis: n.:
the root-canalysis of business problem solving.

Route 66: proper name:
in modern mythology, the *vas deferens* of the nation.

Routine: adj.:
extraordinarily ordinary.

Royalty: n.:
the ideal model for modern governments; the power and perquisites, that is, not the responsiblilities and obligations.

Rule of Law: n.:
one of those high-sounding phrases that means different things in different places: in the USA, it means rule by lawyers; in most of the rest of the world, it means rule by police.

Rum: n.:
the Demon Who Leads Men Astray; source of the family fortunes of half of New England. The finest of the Dionysian diaphoretics.

Run: v.i.:
posture; as to run for public office.

Run the show: phrase:
finish third.

Rush: v.i.:
perform with inadequate time for preparation or proper execution; proceed at an intemperate rate.

n.:
1) an abrupt, addictive, euphoria associated with dosage of certain illicit drugs.
2) a kind of overweight grass that arises from, but remains rooted in, the muck in swamps; occasionally useful a hundred years ago, now used primarily as decoration. In its native environment, it is associated with toxic gases and foul smells.

Russell: v.i.:
make unintelligible noises, usually in the bushes, behind the woodwork, or on PBS.

Rut: n.:
the path down which we pursue our daily lives.
v.i.:
behave like an adolescent.

S

SAD: acronym:
campaign to "Just say No to Sex, Alcohol and Drugs;" aptly named for its prospects for success.

Sabbath: n.:
the holiest day of the week: the one with the most sports programming.

Saccharine: n.:
the characteristic spice of the Disney version.

Sacred: adj.:
important to me.

Sacrifice: v.t.:
give up without hope of immediate return; make holy. Is there a message here?
Something that we always ask others to do, nominally on their own behalf, but preferably on ours.

Saddle bum: n.:
a Britticism in observation of the fact that travel is broadening, even, or, perhaps, especially, on horseback.

Salacious: adj.:
spicy; flavorful. From the Latin for salt, the primordial spice.

Salamander: n.:
a small amphibian often mistaken by the uninitiated for a lizard. Incorrectly identified as a fire lizard or immature dragon, they were believed to be consorts of wizards.

Salary: n.:
modern chains of servitude. Derived from the Latin for "salt", its use evokes images of rubbing salt in the wounds of the week in the trenches.

Sales tax: n.:
value detracting tax.

Salt: v.t.:
to counterfeit the appearance of genuineness or value. Hence, the traditional metaphor of referring to a popular social or political figure as "the salt of the earth."

Saltpeter: n.:
refined guano. Traditional condiment in the kitchens of the military, prisons and all-male schools.

Same-sex marriage: n.:
new political football of the Left vs Right games.
Given normal development, it can be expected to devolve into the traditional form: no-sex marriage.

Sanitary landfill: n.:
a declivity where we dispose of used diapers, rotten food, sewage sludge. etc.

Sanity: n.:
the state of mind exhibited by those who do things my way.

Sanity clause: n.:
provision removed from the Voting Rights Act, lest the candidates be disqualified.

Santa Claus: proper name:
1) to liberals, the proper role of government toward the poor and powerless.
2) to conservatives, the proper role of government toward the corporate world.

Sarcasm: n.:
the poor man's irony.

Sardine: n.:
a pilchard in training to become a mass-transit commuter.

Sardonic: adj.:
in a manner or style appropriate for the evaluation of campaign speeches.

Satan: proper(!) name:
an individual with all the characteristics attributed to a President or Congressman of the other party.

Satire: n.:
an erstwhile literary artform that relied on keen obvservation, acute analysis, and incisive characterization; it has since largely devolved to caricature and cheap shots, with the occasional excursion into lampoon.

Satirist: n.:
a humorist named in honor of the piercing horns and cutting hooves of the goat. The better ones are claimed to share some of the other attributes of *Caper*.

Satyriasis: n.:
extremism…in the pursuit of…

Perpetual emotion in the male.

Scandal: n.:
the result of disclosure of a public figure's private activities.

Scapegoat: n.:
a steed which politicians ride into office and evangelists ride to the bank.

Scatology: n.:
the study of the language of teenagers.

Scenario: n.:
official pipe dream.

Schedule: n.:
freeman's tyrant.

Scholium: n.:
coursework taught in a classroom in an ivory tower.

School: n.:
a very confusing and inconsistent place for young males: when they're 4 or 5, they're told they mustn't go out without their rubbers; 10 years later, they're told they mustn't go in without them.

Schwarzchild: proper name:
a small round country with very secure borders. Immigration is an issue, while out-migration is forbidden.

Schwarzkopf: n.:
German for pimple.

Science: n.:
any collection of anecdotes, assertions, etc. that support my views.

Science of Mind: n.:
pseudoscience of warm-fuzzy, touchy-feely feel-good buzzwords.

Scientific: adj.:
in the law, second-rate. No lawyer will ever let scientific evidence get in the way of a good emotional plea or interfere with tear-jerking anecdotal evidence.

Scientific deduction: n.:
test tube baby.

Scofflaw: n.:
one whose behavior is as though he thinks himself a Congressman.

Scoundrel: n.:
someone more successful than me.

Scruples: n.:
a handicap—inflammation of the conscience gland—which virtually precludes one from a profession in the law or in politics.

Seagull: n.:
amphibious pigeon.

Second: adj.:
losing. In American sports fandom, this position is slightly less respectable than last.

   n.:
one who held the duellist's coat, provided his weapons, tended his wounds, notified his widow…

   v.t.:
in parliamentary usage, to be one of the first to climb onto the bandwagon touoting the matter at question.

The Second American Revolution: n.:
the entirely superfluous declaration by the Republican leadership that they are revolting.
A carefully orchestrated effort to undo all the civil liberties gained in the first one.

Secret: n.:
a precious commodity that provides no satisfaction until shared, at which time it loses that quality which made it precious.

Secret Service: n.:
an agency whose charter is to prosecute purveyors of counterfeit currency and to safeguard purveyors of counterfeit patriotism; the term has evolved to imply clandestine adultery.

Secretary: n.:
the person in an organization with the most real practical power.

"See what you made me do!": phrase:
rallying cry of the professional blamethrower.

Seism: n.:
the doctrine that secrecy is superior to openness.

Seismic: adj.:
earth-shaking.

Self-abuse: n.:
abstemious dysphemism for self-amusement.

Self-control: n.:
self-denial.

Self-discipline: n.:
if discipline is punishment, as most people believe, and punishment is abuse, as the courts now hold, then you figure it out.

Self-fulfilling prophecy: n.:
the kind to specialize in if you want to maintain your prestige as a prophet.

Senate: n.:
one of the two branches of the Legislature, the Senate is referred to as the senior chamber because, unlike the other, they occasionally try to

act as though grown up. Of course, senators have the advantage of not having to run for office every Congress.

Senilia: proper name:
minor Roman goddess, patron of retirement homes.

Sensationalize: v.t.:
edit for presentation on a TV "news magazine."

Sense of humor: n.:
the ability to read jokes from cue cards.

Sense of the Congress: n.:
common oxymoron.

Sensitive: adj.:
over-reactive.

Sentiment: n.:
sentimentality, usually maudlin; the sediment left when we have drained the cup of emotion.

Separate but equal: adj.:
separate.

Separation of Church and State: n.:
a principle that should not be applicable to my church.
Justice Black observed that "a union of government and religion tends to destroy government and to degrade religion." He may have confused cause and effect.

Sequester: v.t.:
to treat a jury less generously than the accused on whom they are to sit in judgement; to imprison without trial or appeal for a sentence of indeterminate length.

Serious proposal: n.:
a negotiating offer designed so as to look good to the press while containing a provision known to be unacceptable to the other side.

Serve: v.t.:
to expend time nonproductively, as a criminal in prison or a politician in office.

Service: v.t.:
attempt to impregnate, as a when bull services a dairy cow to freshen her for milk production. Hence, civil service, service economy.
And what are we to make of "Senior Service" for the Navy?

Sesame Street: n.:
a path for opening the minds of the young; and reopening the minds of the no-longer young.

Sesquipedalian: adj.:
fixated toward utilization of polysyllabic verbiage, especially instances employing obfuscatory vocabulary.

"Set a thief to catch a thief": adage:
the philosophical basis for the selection of chairmen of committees investigating campaign finance irregularities.

Settlement: n.:
the primary obstacle to the establishment of relationships: men aren't willing to settle down, while women aren't willing to "settle for."

Sewer: n.:
a location nearly as neat and sanitary as the mind of a college sophomore.

Sex: n.:

1) America's favorite spectator sport. Frequently confused with violence, which is the core of most of the other popular spectator sports.

    Americans confuse sex and violence so much that rape is still considered a sexual act by most of them.

2) Man's favorite substitute for love.

In spite of our cultural ambivalence about the relation between the acts of sex and love, "Go love yourself" has never been known to be an effective insult.

Sexual harassment: n.:
unwanted or embarassing attention of a kind associated with male courting or courting-display behaviors. Not to be confused with unwanted or embarassing attention of a kind associated with female courting or courting-display behaviors, which shall be considered to be constitutionally protected free speech.

Sexism: n.:
any attitude or activity that does not exalt females.

Sexist: n.:
adult white male.
>adj.:
having the property shared by all general statements about females.

Shame: n.:
irritating exudation of the conscience gland.

Share: v.t.:
new-age-ese for tell. Used to imply (usually falsely) that the listener gives a damn.

Shark: n.:
a cold-blooded predator with an insatiable appetite for destruction and consumption; lawyer of the sea.

Shiite: n.:
a religious sect whose name is two letters longer than the description of its leadership.

Ship: n.:
commercial conveyance of a scope to be launched by one millihelen. Original attribution probably not by Homer, but by another blind Attic poet of the same name.

Shooting gallery: n.:
1) overseas Marine posting.

2) a) a recreational facility adulated and encouraged by the NRA and their allies and friends;

b) a recreational facility denigrated and discriminated against by the NRA and their allies and friends.

Show the flag: clause:
"mine is bigger than yours" played on a national scale, usually as a means of forcing foreign policy.

Shrew: n.:
a small mammal noted for its ferocity, voracity and venomous bite; a nagging wife. The latter variety can be tamed.

Shroud: n.:
ultimate wardrobe.

Shyster: n.:
crooked lawyer; lawyer.

Silent Majority: n.:
the graveyard vote.

Silicone Valley: name:
artificially enhanced cleavage.

Silk purse: n.:
cause of deafness in pigs.

Silver: n.:
a metal with remarkable medical value: it is noteworthy for its ability to treat itching of the palm. Dosage should be carefully controlled,

however, as the taking of a mere thirty pieces can do overwhelming damage to one's reputation. Note: habit forming.

Simulated: adj.:
phony.

Simulation: n.:
the con man's—or the computer's—version.

Sin: n.:
1) anything you do that I would be ashamed or afraid to do.
2) an offense against God, which must be avenged by His chosen here on Earth.

To most of those whose doctrines include sin, the worst sin is that of getting caught.

Sincerity: n.:
the most overrated of virtues—all the sincerity in the world won't make you right.
Often confused with "honesty", to which it bears no relationship.

Siren song: n.:
an irresistible appeal; from the way crowds form around any use of the siren by emergecy vehicles.

Sissy: n.:
man who acts feminine, especially one who wears women's clothes. Explain this to the next Highlander in his kilt that you encounter.

Sisyphus: proper name:
the figure in Greek mythology who never can do it right and always must do it over.

Sitcom: n.:
the medium through which Hollywood TV executives express their respect for the intelligence and sensitivity of their audiences, and the

quality of their writers, by feeling it necessary to tell the viewer when he is supposed to laugh.

Ski: v.i.:
perform one of two categories of snow-borne athletic activity:
1) Nordic, or cross-country, which is patterned after an exercise designed to strengthen the lungs and heart;
2) Alpine, or downhill, which is an exercised designed to break legs and blow out knees.

Skinhead: n.:
another example of the deplorable spelling abilities of our time, though they got the form right: s-<consonant>-i-<consonant>-head.

Slander: n.:
word-of-mouth advertising; libel for illiterates.

Slang: n.:
the Vulgate Dictionary.

Slant: v.t.:
to write an article such that the message is not what I would want conveyed.

Slash: v.t.:
treat with the same tender consideration that Republicans show to social-program funding.

Slaver: n.:
the agent, usually black or Arab, from whom the European slave traders acquired their goods.

Slavery: n.:
indentured servitude, open-ended and attested by a third party.

Sleep: n.:
Nature's answer to the problem of Monday.

Slick Willy: epithet:
Oxford slang for a recently withdrawn member.

Slippery slope: n.:
the surface the camel stands on as he sticks his nose into your tent; paved with good intentions.

Sloppy: adj.:
having the esthetic appeal of the contents of the chamberpot; barely fit to throw to the hogs.

Slug: n.:
homeless escargot.

Smog: n.:
industrial-strength air.

Smoke-filled room: n.:
number one on the Surgeon General's hit list until AIDS came along to promote sex to that slot.
Tradidional smoke-filled rooms are more dangerous to those outside them than to those inside them.

Smoking gun: n.:
the ultimate Liberal insult, being comprised of "smoking", a reprehensible vice, and "gun", the modern demon.

Smuggler: n.:
Libertarian importer.

Snail: n.:
unofficial mascot of the Postal Service.

Snide: adj.:
tending to attack without warning, from below and behind.

Snipe: n.:
a marsh bird hunted by preadolescent males in a rite of passage.
    v.i.:

attack using a weapon slightly more acute than a bludgeon, preferably from a safe distance or vantage.

Snob: n.:
1) an insecure oaf, deathly afraid that noone will recognize their superiority if they act human.
2) an arrogant fool who considers his station superior to mine.

Snow: v.t.:
wave the hands rapidly enough to create the confusing effect of a blizzard. The authentic product of a snow is white, while that of the handwaving type is a pastoral brown.

   n.:
symbolically, anything white. "If there's snow on the roof, that doesn't mean the fire's out in the furnace" is a popular motto among upper-middle aged men. If there's snow on the roof and the fire's not out in the furnace, it shows that the roof is well insulated. The body insulates itself with blubber.

Soap opera: n.:
one of a family of ongoing narratives of sex, infidelity, treachery and criminality to which the bulk of opponents to pornography and of sex and violence on television are addicted.

Social: adj.:
unable to be effective when trying to operate solo.

Society: n.:
a subset of the populace, distinguished by some common interest or attribute, especially power, prestige and status. Hence, sociology, the study of the dynamics of society.

Solar power: n.:
an energy-supply system that won't be widely promoted until the government figures out how to tax sunshine or the oil companies figure out how to bill for its use.

Solicitation: n.:
enticement to ill-advised action; as solicitation of prostitution, solicitation of funds for charity, solicitation of government grants.

Solicitor: n.:
in the USA, a licensed panhandler; in the UK, a lawyer not admitted to argue before the court.

Somatotype: n.:
human body styles.
There are three basic somatotypes:
1) ectomorph: built like a marathoner, basketball player or fashion model. This type lives longest statistically, so they form the basis for the height-weight tables in the health books.
2) mesomorph: built like Charles Atlas; the prototype jock build.
3) endomorph: built like the Pillsbury Doughboy. Statistically, this type is likeliest to be associated with chronic illness.

These patterns lead those who can't tell cause from effect to take up arms in their War On Portliness.

Some Assembly Required: phrase:
the Ghost of Christmas Present.
Congratulations, you have just volunteered to become the unpaid employee of the company you bought the toy from.

Songbird: n.:
denizen of the commons noted for its cheerful voice and its habit of spotting cars.

Sordid: adj.:
suitable for inclusion in a soap opera or a TV movie.

"The sorriest spectacle it has ever been my misfortune to witness:" phrase:
the other side won.

Soul: n.:
supernatural attribute connected to a person at conception, at birth or at baptism, depending on religion.
   adj.:
African-american. A supernatural attribute assigned to food, music, ill-mannered behavior, etc., to place them outside the range of White experience.

Sound bite: n.:
advertising jingle of political marketing; the huckster's version of the aphorism.

The Sound of Music: phrase:
what the hills are alive with: mosquitoes, ticks, off-road vehicles... Maybe Schoenberg and the others were right, after all.

Space program: n.:
America's contribution to our attempt to rise from the cradle of the race.
Brought to prominence by John Kennedy, it has never recovered from its revitalization under the Nixon administration.

Spare parts: n.:
the only potential social value of a lot of those idiots running around out there.

Speaker of the House: n.:
preeminent noise source in the Congress.
Punch in the parliamentary puppet show.

Spear carrier: n.:
operatic performer whose relation to the star is as yours to me.
When you have the feeling that the meaning of your life is to be a spear carrier in the story of someone else's life, the condition is either depression or devotion.

Special: adj.:
retarded; defective; inadequate; noncompetitive.

Special interest: n.:
him, if you're my friend; you, if you're not.

Special rights: n.:
basic civil rights for someone I dislike.

Specialize: v.i.:
to constrain one's scope of inquiry narrowly enough to allow some chance of gaining expertise in one's lifetime.
The ultimate goal of specialization is to be able to master everything about nothing at all.

Specialty: n.:
an area where one has enough expertise to successfully hoodwink the uninitiated.

Specie: n.:
hard money; now extinct in the United States, except for a very few showcase pieces of value primarily to collectors, and for a few relict cartwheels used by the casinos.

Species: n.:
any grouping of non-human life that is identifiable enough for environmental activists to use as grounds for a lawsuit under the Endangered Species act.

Specious: adj.:
sharing the fundamental quality of species-ist arguments.

Spectacular: adj.:
1) featuring lots of stars and choreography.
2) suitable for use as the basis of a mini-series.

Spectator: n.:
voyeur.

Speech: n.:
a public performance wherein the speaker, using very many words, says nothing.
The after-dinner speech is the northern equivalent of the tropical *siesta* after meals.

Spike: v.t.:
(of traffic) to cause a lane of traffic to flow more slowly by the act of changing into it.
    n.:
Brad, on steroids.

Spin doctor: n.:
one whose job it is to twist the meaning or perception of a gaffe; the political equivalent of the guy who makes balloons into animals at fairs and childrens' parties.
The spin doctor at the White House usually does a good imitation of a Dervish.

Spiritual leader: n.:
one who teaches to his followers the virtue of giving up wealth. They are taught to give it up to him.

Spite: n.:
the most accomplished—and accomplishing—of the human emotions.

Spock: proper name:
1) the hero of a generation of parents, who gave them permission to avoid the difficult act of teaching discipline to their children.
2) the hero of a generation of children, who gave them permission to base their behavior on their logic more than on their feelings.

Sponsored research: n.:
classically, the story of the Glory Hound *vs.* the Greed Head.

Spontaneous: adj.:
carefully scripted so as to sound unrehearsed.

Spontaneous combustion: n.:
self-motivation of the igneous persuasion.

Sport: n.:
(preferably violent) physical activity presented for our amusement.

Sportsmanship: n.:
graciousness and discipline associated with competitive activity, the reason given for expending tax dollars on high-school and collegiate sports. The young players are taught sportsmanship by such luminaries of the art as Bobby Knight and Woody Hayes.

Spotted owl: n.:
stalking horse of the eco-activist in his war to stamp out primary industry; scapegoat of the sylvan harvest industry to account for the inevitable consequences of generations of greed and mismanagement.

Spy: n.:
footsoldier in the nonshooting wars between states.
v.i.:
observe carefully without permission, as an industry on its rivals, a parent on her children, or a government on it citizens.

Square: adj.:
1) generational slang for dull, uninteresting, stodgy, undesirable;
2) honest.

Squeal: n.:
the only part of the hog never found in hot dogs.

Squire: n.:
Queenly honorific for the sort of man who would choose to wear a really bad hairpiece.

Staff officer: n.:
    professional soldier studying to learn how to fight the last war.

Star: n.:
    a celestial orb that shines by its own light, or a human who thinks he does.
    Astronomical stars are far above and beyond the everyday concerns of men; human stars act as though they believe they are, too.

Star Chamber: n.:
    prototype of the National Security Council.

Star Wars: n.:
    an heroic venture in a time long ago and a galaxy far away, but only there and then.

Starr: n.:
    veterinary specialist: equino-proctologist.

Starr Chamber: n.:
    a place for the subornation of witnesses, especially in the course of fishing expeditions.

Stars and Bars: n.:
    emblem of a country within a nation, dedicated to the proposition that all white Protestant men are created equal, and everyone else can take potluck.

Stars and Stripes: phrase:
    emblem of the nation, standard to the patriot; icon to the right.

State of the Union: phrase:
    overdrawn.

Statesman: n.:
    an honorific bestowed on dead politicians; hence the tendency to observe, in times of crisis, the need for more statesmen.

Statesmanship: n.:
the ability to maintain a straight face while pronouncing platitudes.

Statistics: n.:
the most widely published and read variety of Science Fiction.

Steal: v.t.:
appropriate without writ.

Steatopygia: n.:
a condition pertinent to Hottentots, where it's adaptive, and middle managers, where it's pygalgic.

Steer: n.:
taurine eunuch. Hence, any male made tractable by removal of the organs of aggression.

v.t.:

1) control the direction and attitude of.

2) prepare for being controlled in direction and attitude.

Steganography: n.:
the art of hiding information in plain sight, after the fashion of Poe's "Purloined Letter." This has become popular in the computer age for embedding serial-number information in images, etc. The practice of hiding information by dispersing it among many words of data was probably inspired by observation of the practices of software manual writers.

Stem to stern: phrase:
front to back, on a ship or a man.

Stereotype: n.:
the mold we use when we cast a person as a scapegoat.

Steroids: n.:
artificial male hormones; taken by guys who think their balls aren't big enough to make all the genuine male hormones they need to be successful.

Stock market: n.:
Wall Street's generous provision for those who haven't the free time to go to Las Vegas or Atlantic City on workdays.

Stockholder: n.:
one of a member of the distributed ownership of a company: one of those who can expect to be left holding the bag after the executives have had their way with the company.

"Stop the presses": phrase:

1) the Prohibitionists' message to the vintner.

2) Nixon's response to the publishing of the Pentagon Papers.

Stout: adj.:
euphemistically fat

Straight and narrow: adj phrase:
the Right mindset.

Straw man: n.:
the debater's favorite opponent.

Strict Constructionist: n.:
a jurist who desires to rebuild the Constitution with all the weight shifted to the right.

Strike: n.:

1) the only activity that is performed in common by professional athletes in all the major televised sports.

2) the basic action of professional baseball.

Strike out: v.i.:
the only thing in baseball the average teenage boy does as well as a major-leaguer.

Struggle: v.i.:
attempt to stave off, or at least delay, the inevitable.

Strumpet: n.:
a woman who has found her livelihood in her niche.

Sturgeon's Law: n.:
"Ninety percent of everything is crap."
Sturgeon was a notorious optimist.

Style: n.:
a technique for rendering goods socially valueless before they become physically worthless.

Subclinical: adj.:
said of a medical condition not severe enough to put you in the hospital.

Subjectivity: n.:
an affliction which renders the sufferer unable to see things from my perspective.

Submarine: n.:
heroic sandwich. Their races are a favorite spectator sport of high-school and college students.

Subpoena: n.:
an excretion of the Body Politic, in its incarnation as justiciar.

Subsidy: n.:
robbing Peter to pay Paul, if Peter is a taxpayer and Paul is a special interest group.

Success: n.:
the result required to make speculation respectable.

Successful: adj.:
having achieved the status of target for acquisitive lawyers and their greedy clients, and for petty journalists and the generally disaffected.

Suicide: n.:
taking control of one's life for the last time; considered a sin by those who deny the right to take control of one's own life and a crime by those who mistrust the First Amendment.
Suicide is considered a crime by most supporters of capital punishment. Unfortunately, not a capital crime.

Suit: n.:
1) the primary mechanism by which lawyers exert their parasitism on Society;

2) the sort of functionary whose job allows him to show up for work in a $700 suit, and go home with it unruined; typically a parasite on the productive in Business.

Sunshine: n.:
fallout from the thermonuclear reactor that runs 90-odd percent of the whole show.
Nature's own antidepressant, especially in winter; addictive and potentially toxic.

Super: adj.:
slightly more unusual than the average.

Super Bowl: n.:
a ceremonial augury used to forecast the following year's activity in the Stock Market.

Superconductor: n.:
the Leonard Bernstein of metals.

Superficial: adj.:
as deep and penetrating as a political ad or a network news story.

Superior morality: n.:
1) my morality.
2) bigger battalions.

Superlative: n.:
the fat with which the stuff of advertising is larded.

Supernova: n.:
an astronomical entity nearly as bright as my grandchild.

Supply side economics: n.:
I've got mine and now I want you to give me most of yours, in hopes that you might get a little of it back later.

Support and defend: v.t.:
ignore; from observation of the behavior of Congressmen, who are sworn to support and defend the Constitution.

Surf: v.t.:
ride, with pretentions to mastery: as the kahuna, the wave; the sailboarder, the wind; the nerd, the Net (more recently, the Web); or the couch potato, the channels of his remote control.

Surgeon: n.:
the cutup in the operating room.

Surgeon General: n.:
the Government's doctor; he orders you not to get sick. The primary consideration of the job description seems to be to lower the potential liability of health insurers.

Surplusage: n.:
the mark of a writer being paid by the word.

Surprise: n.:
the emotion elicited by the discovery that a public official has actually told the truth.

Survival of the fittest: n phrase:
a descriptive biological phenomenon coopted as a prescriptive social dogma, by the successful as an excuse for their ruthlessness.

Survivalism: n.:
a doctrine of "I've got mine—the rest of you are fair game;" sort of a traditional Babbitt-esque Republicanism reduced to its lowest form.

Survivalist: n.:
one whose self-styled military and self-sufficiency skills assure him that he will be one of the survivors of a cataclysm, while they reassure us that he won't.

Swashbuckling: adj.:
flamboyantly or irresponsibly combative, as American foreign policy in the 80's.

Swearing: n.:
pyrotechnic, self-illuminating language. It doesn't solve any problems, but it can surely relieve the symptoms.

Sweeps week: n.:
the culminating effort of the TV networks. So called because of the way they sweep judgement, quality and good taste under the rug.

Sweet: adj.:
cloying.

Sweet reason: n.:
logic that has the desirable property of supporting my beliefs.

Swing: v.i.:
1) play a style of dance-band music popular with the young and active generation of World War II;
2) partake of a social-marital activity popular with the same generation 20 years later.

Sybaritic: adj.:
decorated in the style of the Senate Office Building or a Las Vegas casino.

Sycophancy: n.:
the art of congratulating someone more powerful on how much he is as we should wish to be.

Sycophant: n.:
one who behaves as a fawning dog; the insecure person's fondest friend.
Applicant for appointive office.

Syllable: n.:
element of a word. More than two in a given word leads to confusion.

Syllogism: n.:
a method in formal logic consisting of a major presumption, a minor presumption and a forgone conclusion.

Symmetry: n.:
fancy word for "everything's got to balance."

Symptom: n.:
what we treat when it would require an effort to remove the disease.

Syncopation: n.:
poetry in the language of rhythm.

Syncretist: n.:
one who dulls the edges of oxymorons and unravels paradoxes.

Syndicate: n.:
a association of businesses or businessmen convoked for the purpose of acting like a Prohibition-era gang.

Syndrome: n.:
medical term meaning "we can't identify a cause for why you're ill."

Synopsis: n.:
a condensation that retains the important points.
A good synopsis bears the same relation to its original that a cup of stock bears to the chicken: it retains the essential character while sacrificing the texture.

Syphilis: n.:
Montezuma's Real Revenge.

T

T & A: n. phrase:
Titillation and Assininity; the currency of the advertising trade.

Tab: n.:
1) a protrusion that makes identification and location of something easier.
2) a line of credit that makes identification and location of someone necessary.

Tabloid: n.:
a newspaper whose content will only be improved on by its being used to line a parrot's cage.
All the news that's not fit to print.

Tabu: n.:
any act that would raise Mrs Grundy's eyebrows.

Tabula rasa: n.:
a document listing the positive accomplishments of a session of Congress.

Tact: n.:
the ability to step on someone's toes without bruising their ego.

Tail wagging the dog: *gerundive* phrase:
US foreign policy since World War II.

Take Back America: phrase:
impose an ideology on the body politic which it has never before had to bear.

Taking care of business: phrase:
Contract with America.

Talent: n.:
the discriminator between performer and artist.

Talk is cheap: phrase:
1) the dream of every campaign finance manager.

2) an obsolete sentiment from before the Bell breakup.

3) a sentiment widely held before C-Span.

Talk radio: n.:
the Wasteland of Rant. Divided between those who seek to shock by the use of obscene language and those who seek to shock with obscene ideas.

Tan: v.i.:
turn skin to leather.

Tantalus: proper name:
figure in Greek mythology who is condemned to have his heart's desire held just out of reach. Kind of like Harold Stassen or Norman Thomas and the Presidency; or George Bush and the second term.

Tao: n.:
the religion of millions of Chinese; compare with the homonymous "Dow," the religion of millions of Republicans.

Tar: n.:
the active ingredient in highway pavement, cigarette smoke and certain baseball bats.

Tar Baby: proper name:
Joel Harris's tribute to the institution of the political record.

Tariff: n.:
the government's jack; used for tipping playing fields.

Task force: n.:
the title a committee affects when they want to sound aggressive.

Taste: n.:
that character of the American public that noone ever went broke by underestimating.

Tasteless: adj.:
1) having the savor of a primetime TV show—or an old Benny Hill episode.
2) showing the esthetic discrimination of an in-law.

Tattoo: n.:
portable art.

Tautology: n.:
superfluous redundancy. Phrases such as "sex pervert" (what other kind do we have?) or "shower activity" (vs inactive rain?) which are used to fill time or sound pompous. Are news writers paid by the word?
Liberals would include "police brutality," while conservatives would consider "welfare cheat" to be a member of the set.

Tavern: n.:
a place where men go to drink to get stiff and women go to drink to get tight, whence they leave together to discover that neither is either.

Tax: v.t.:

1) rob with government sanction.

2) stress close to the limit.

Tax cut: n.:

the political equivalent of the candy offered to a child to get them to get into the car.

Tax equity: n.:

from each according to my ideology, to each according to my view of his need.

Tax evasion: n.:

the French national sport.

Much more popular in the USA than that other French institution, the Metric System.

Taxation without representation: n.:

deficit spending.

If this seems strange, ask any grade-schooler, who will spend his life paying off the debt run up by those now in power.

Apart from the periodic circuses called elections, taxation without representation is not easily distinguishable from taxation with representation.

Team: n.:

1) a gang involved in activities which have my approval.

2) a committee with leadership (rare)(very rare).

Tease: v.t.:

cause another's reach to exceed their grasp, so they can never quite have what they have been led to desire.

Technically: adv.:

1) through a loophole.

2) to a nit picker.

Technobabble: n.:
sequences of language using scientific-sounding words, but without substance or meaning; as the scripts of science fiction shows, the pronouncements of creationists, or the legal arguments of consumer advocates.

Technological leadership: n.:
possession of a marketing department adept at coining buzzwords and evoking memorable, if vaguely related, imagery to publicize their product.

Teeth: n.:
1) enforcement authority, as a "law with teeth in it."
2) the natural resource that is mined to support dentists.
Dentists have a saying: "Just ignore problems with your teeth and they'll go away."

Telecon: n.:
'phone solicitor who got caught.

Telephone: n.:
a Quisling servant that lets salesmen and other vermin into our homes.

Telescope: n.:
the heretic instrument, which caused more dislocation in the Church than anything before or since.

Televangelist: n.:
a preacher who has exchanged his sackcloth and ashes for cashmere and Max Factor.

Television: n.:
the most potent and dangerous mind-altering substance yet devised by the hand of Man.

Temper: n.:
in tools, the measure of the ability to avoid breaking; in tool users, the measure of the tendency to break from control.

Temptation: n.:
the irresistible force.

Tenure: n.:
a vaccination that gives academics lifetime immunity to the vicissitudes of the law of supply and demand.

Term limits: n.:
Washington's way of giving control of the government back to the voters: by telling them that they can't vote for people who have held office long enough to learn how to do the job.
Interestingly enough, they ignore the fact that the voters have the opportunity to limit terms already: every two years for the House and every six for the Senate.
It is also interesting to note that the activists pushing term limits legislation always point with scorn to Ted Kennedy, and never to Jesse Helms or Strom Thurmond.

Term of office: n.:
the time between the promises and the alibis.

Terminal illness: n.:

1) the Amtrak disease; contagious, look at Greyhound.

2) excessive belief in the Information SuperHighway.

3) breathing.

Terminally shy: adj phrase:
computerphobic.

Territory: n.:
map. Specifically, the map drawn by my people.

Terrorism: n.:
use of force in support of a cause that I don't support.

Testicles: proper name:
minor, one might say dependent, Greek god; patron deity of weight lifters.

Testosterone: n.:
the hormone which in overabundance may cause a man to act as though he had PMS.

Testy: adj.:
manifesting behaviors characteristic of overactive testes.
The usage of referring to male aggression hormones isn't just poetic license.

THC: n.:
magic substance used by the Beat Generation as a substitute for TLC, with which most are unacquainted and/or incapable.

Thanks: n.:
a platitude offered to someone when we have taken him for all we can get away with, so as to dispose him favorably toward our next expedition.

Theater of the absurd: n.:
any high-profile criminal trial in the modern American legal system.

Theme park: n.:
a multi-acre full-time commercial that you pay to attend.

Theocracy: n.:
government by Divine pronouncement.
Democrats would say this is the Republican political platform.

Theoretically: adv.:
if I had my way…

Theory: n.:
a guess that has done its homework.

"There is absolutely nothing to be afraid of.": clause:
be afraid. Be very, very afraid.

Thesaurus: n.:
the most erudite of the dinosaurs.

Thespian: n.:
an actor who is better than he should be.

Thief: n.:
a scoundrel who took something I wanted.

Think tank: n.:
a planning organization named in recognition of the quality of their thoughts; the tank in question traditionally has a chain attached.

Third Reich: n.:
the "Thousand Year Reich." Apparently, that problem Germany had with inflation affected more than just their money.

Thought: n.:
the realm where we can be the equal of any; the only realm.
Of the triad, word, thought and deed, the one that can be private.

Thought police: n.:
officials who tell you you can go to jail for what you're thinkin'.
A legacy of George Orwell—the word, not the phenomenon; that's been around at least as long as there have been priests—or gossips.

Three Laws of Thermodynamics: n.:
1) you can't win;
2) you can't break even;
3) you can't get out of the game.

Three ring circus: n.:
a low public spectacle comprising the prosecution's table, the defense's table and the press pool.

Three-time loser: n.:
voter in a constituency with a third-term legislator.

"Throw the rascals out": motto:
vote the scoundrels in.

Time: n.:
money. Or, since the days of Einstein, space.

Timid: adj.:
observing life in accordance with the adage: "nothing ventured, nothing lost."

Tin Pan Alley: n.:
the fertile field wherein popular music was grown for some fifty years. Too much rock left it barren.

"To err is human": phrase:
I messed up again.

"To make a long story short": phrase:
to make a long story even longer…

Toad: n.:
1) collector of toadies.
2) a small, dry amphibian which bears a frightening resemblance to an in-law.

Toast: n.:
liquid epigram.

Tobacco: n.:
according to the US Surgeon General, the weapon with which the Indian has killed more white men than he ever managed to with arrow or tomahawk.

Tofu: n.:
Chinese cheese, bland, pale and milkfree.

Tolerance: n.:
social incendiary; any small demonstration of tolerance is enough to ignite any fundamentalist.
Formerly, tolerance of other races, religions or cultural practices was sufficient to cause deflagration. These have been superseded by tolerance of sexual variation as the most pyrophoric behaviors.

Tomb: n.:
a small apartment wherein to dwell in the days after your final days.

Tome: n.:
reading matter for pedants and poseurs.

Topical humor: n.:
news datelined Washington D.C.

Topologist: n.:
a mathematician who doesn't know the difference between a donut, a cup of coffee, and the man that consumes both.

Tornado: n.:
whirlwind of great intensity; mysteriously attracted to mobile home parks.
Scientists say tornadoes are caused by hot air rising.
The Bible says "they have sown the wind, and they shall reap the whirlwind."
The pattern of tornado activity follows the pattern of ascendancy of fundamentalist and evangelical church acitivity in the United States.

Tort: n.:
lawyerese for a harm done to me.

Tort reform: n.:
financial armor for those with adequate finances.

Total commitment: n.:
any level of involvement that entails more than learning a couple of slogans.

Totem: n.:
an element of Nature, usually an animal, believed by primitive peoples to embody or represent the collective spirit of the community. Not to be confused with a mascot, which is an animal chosen by a sports team to symbolize the collective spirit of the fans.

Tough on crime: motto:
tough on non-white-collar and non-white-skin crime.

Trade deficit: n.:
grass roots foreign aid.

Traditional: adj.:
the way I remember we did it when I was a kid.

Tragedy: n.:
in theater, when the hero doesn't get the girl; in life, when he does.

Tragic: adj.:
suitable for use as the basis for an appeal for emergency relief funds.

Traitor: n.:
one who has shifted allegiances away from mine.

Transparent: adj.:
something even I can see through.

Travel: n.:
popular excuse for going off the diet; hence the maxim: travel is broadening.

Travesty: n.:
a verdict I didn't want and didn't expect.

Treachery: n.:
application of the principle of *laissez faire* in the realm of politics.

Treason: n.:
espousal of positions more liberal than the government approves of. Once on a time, giving aid and comfort to an enemy constituted treason. In the 1980s, either declaring war on the US did not make one an enemy, selling arms to an enemy did not constitute giving aid, or we lived in more forgiving times.

Trial in the press: phrase:
Everyone is assumed innocent until accused.
A spate of high-profile and celebrity court cases have succeded in driving the quality of court reportage even lower than it has been for medical and scientific matters.

Triangle: n.:
the eternal form. Lucky Pierre's favorite shape.

Triathlon: n.:
the going-for-times that try mens' soles.

Trinity: n.:
1) Unity.

2) the antithesis of Unity.

In these forms, it is the core and dividing property of Christianity.

3) Man's first use of Hellfire.

Tripp: v.t.:
betray; stumble

Trivialization: n.:
inflation, as it applies to language or the law. The popular current usages of "rape", "sexual harassment", "child abuse", etc., are the linguistic equivalent of trillion-dollar rolls of toilet paper.

Trivialize: v.t.:
edit for presentation on the Evening News.

Trojan horse: n.:
  1) an attractive wrapper with an unpleasant filling, rather like some chocolates, or many candidates.
  2) model for very large condoms.
  a computer program based on the same principles as the advertising for computer programs: promise one thing and deliver something entirely different.

Tropical humor: n.:
  elephant jokes.

Truce: n.:
  time out to reload.

True: adj.:
  widely believed, especially if I believe it.

Truth: n.:
  1) what I said.
  2) what I want to be.
  3) (capitalized) a mythical quality, supposed to be a fundamental property of the Universe.

Truth in advertising: phrase:
  nothing works better; we don't make any money selling nothing.

Truth In Advertising Act: n.:
  commercial equivalent of the Ethics In Government Act: a piece of light fiction designed for the amusement of high-school Civics classes, honored in the breach more than in the observance.

Tsunami: n.:
  seismic sea wave: a (sometimes big) ripple caused by an earthquake. The term was coined to replace the inaccurate "tidal wave," which is an entirely unrelated phenomenon that occasionally presents a similar appearance.

"Tsunami" is Japanese for tidal wave.

Tunnel: n.:
primary source of political vision.

Turn on the Juice: phrase:
what the press did, following the lead of the L.A. DA's office.

Twaddle: n.:
the content of advertisements, sermons, political speeches or legal briefs, inter alia.

Two-faced: adj.:
having the rudimentary qualification for the law or politics.

Two-party system: n.:

1) a party which owns more than one candidate.

2) that political institution which in each election year brings us the traditional evil of the two lessers.

Two-scoops: adj.:
as flakey as a box of raisin bran.

Typewriter: n.:
a demonic device which has cast a curse on the quality of handwriting in the modern world.

Tyrannosaurus: n.:
the most beloved of the dinosaurs; his disposition would have suited him well for twentieth-century culture; that and the size of his brain would suggest a career in the law or politics.

Tyranny: n.:
government I don't like.

U

Ugly: adj.:
 showing the esthetic qualities of her children or my in-laws; what no baby is, to a politician, in public.

Ulster: proper name:
 the state in Great Britain which most eloquently epitomizes the Christian principles of brotherly love and tolerance.

Ultraconservative: adj.:
 descriptive of a moderate Iranian, or a member of the Reagan cabinet.

Ultranationalism: n.:
 the Republican Revolution.

Unaccountable: adj.:
 beyond my ability to explain easily; as, why does the average bathroom have more favorable acoustics than the great concert halls?

Unavailable for comment: adj. phrase:
 unwilling to talk to us.

Uncivil: adj.:
 behaving after the fashion of a civil servant.

Uncle: n.:
1) a cry of children, given in despair to denote acceptance of defeat.
2) the nickname of the government.

Unconscious: adj.:
showing the level of awareness of one's surroundings that Congressmen show of their constituents' needs.

Uncountable: adj.:
greater than the number of tokens available in the society; a class of numbers developed in response to the need to reimburse such authors as Dickens, Hugo, Fielding, Dostoevski on a by-the-word basis.

Under the influence: phrase:
over the limit.

Under the knife: adv phrase:
recreational locale for Lotte Lenya.

Underground economy: n.:
the one that takes place out of the sight of the IRS and (most of) the banks; so named for where you end up if you miss your payments.

Underrated: adj.:
in the market for a new PR agent. Most frequently used of athletes.

Understanding: n.:
the condition of having learned a bit of something well enough to be able to parrot it at appropriate times.
The father of Conflict.

Undervalued: adj.:
cheap.

Unforgiveable sin: n.:
any offense against me or violation of my closely held tenets.

Uniform: adj.:
 not exhibiting variation.
  n.:
 not allowing variation.

Union: n.:
 a self-marketing organization for wage slaves.

Unique: adj.:
 having some property or characteristic which is distinguishable from the run of the mill.

United Nations: n.:
 an ongoing demonstration that the human race is not ready for self government.
 Fortunately for the human race, we have lawyers, politicians, warlords and theocrats.

Universal: adj.:
 applicable to me, and a couple of others.

Unjust: adj.:
 not on my social agenda.

Unlawful: n.:
 in the fashion of most drug, espionage or terrorist investigations.

Unspoiled: adj.:
1) (of people) a) not yet aligned with my opponents; b) not yet exposed to the attractions of my opponents.
2) (of Nature) not yet exposed to me.

Unsung hero: n.:
 obsolete term for a good guy who didn't toot his own horn. Given the modern trends in heroes—Calley, North, etc.—any unhung hero is now noteworthy.

Unusual: adj.:
outside my daily experience; not what I expected.

Unwieldy: adj.:
large enough to make the managers work a little.

Up: adv.:
what down looks like, when you've been there long enough.

Upper: n.:
how the Depression generation face the morning.
Self-discipline in a brown bottle for the would-be dieter.

Upwind: adj.:
the side to stand when taking in a campaign speech.

Urban development: n.:
what we have now that Mrs. O'Leary and her cow have been banished to agricultural zones.

Urologist: n.:
doctor who makes a business of looking up your business.

User-friendliness: n.:
the Holy Grail of computer products designers—oft sought, never found. The desire for user-friendliness so permeates the field that they frequently miscall a bus a buss, which is a very much friendlier device.

Utility: n.:
a business enterprise that has been granted a monopoly over something particularly useful.

Utopia: proper name:
The perfect land, whose capital is named Shangri-La; the land which can never be; the land that every politician promises in his or her campaign speeches.

V

Vacant: adj.:
unoccupied, but not necessarily empty. Examples include the lot where the neighborhood kids play ball and the gaze of the date who is thinking about someone else entirely.

Vacation: n.:
a period of time when you worry about the problems of work without having the information or tools available to deal with them.

Vacuum: n.:
something that is disgusting to Nature. Most bachelors don't seem to like them very much, either.

Value: n.:
the return something will garner in the marketplace. Hence the conservative emphasis on "family values."

Value added tax: n.:
a scheme that raises the price and lowers the value of everything proportionally to its worth.

Vanity: n.:
the force that attracts us to mirrors.

Vapid: adj.:
rated G.

Vaudeville: n.:
traditional home of the vaudevillain, purveyor of titillation and tasteless entertainment. No longer functional, its place has been taken by the daytime talk show, the sitcom and the political campaign.

Vegetarian: n.:
cereal killer; one who has determined that the life of a cow or a fish is sacred while that of a carrot or a potato is not.

Venal: adj.:
a type of sin which is not mortal, as opposed to venial sin, which, since the advent of AIDS, may well be mortal.

Verb: n.:
noun.
Nero Wolfe would refuse further conversation with anyone who used "impact" or "contact" as verbs. This totally cut him off from the Yuppies, who were nearly the only ones with enough money to afford his fees.

Verbalize: v.t.:
use a noun or an adjective as a verb.

Vermillion: adj.:
the color of ink used for recording the US Budget: deep, deep red.

Veto: v.t.:
If we can't play it my way, nobody's going to play at all.
The Russian spelling is transliterated "Nyet."

Viable: adj.:
not (quite) stillborn.

Vice: n.:
an activity you enjoy and I don't approve of: evil, wickedness, depravity; hence, Vice President, Vice Chairman, Vice Admiral, etc. The Vice President is the President of the Senate; the Senate is considered to be the superior chamber of the Congress. This pretty well defines the value of Congress.

Vice President: n.:
ventriloquist's dummy to the executive branch.

Victim: n.:
the one to blame for a calamity.

Victimless crime: n.:
benevolent government's means of protecting you from yourself.

Victor: n.:
1) the candidate with the fewest votes against him.

2) the one who gets to write the history.

Vietnam: n.:
symbol of the middle-American dream: guilt without sex.

Viking: n.:
first-millenium Norseman or Dane on furlough during the off season between planting and harvest.

Vindicate: v.t.:
provide a politically acceptable excuse.

Violence: n.:
physical oppression, the legal use of which is restricted to the government and military.
The first refuge of the incompetent.
Always simulated in entertainment, and usually in sport, because the real thing is uninteresting to watch and is over too quickly to garner good ratings.

A punster's favorite section of the orchestra.

Violent crime: n.:
title of the campaign to justify suspension of police controls, which replaced drug trafficking when that campaign foundered.

Virgin: adj.:
unsullied by contact with humans, especially male humans.

Virgin wool: n.:
product of Little Bo Peep's flock.

Virtual: adj.:
illusory; unreal. As virtual community, virtual reality.

Virtue: n.:
1) any transgression that has been routinely committed long enough to have become generally accepted or expected.
2) behavior by others in accordance with the dictates of my conscience.

A self-rewarding activity which in general is much more rewarding to the observer than the practitioner.

Virtuous: adj.:
exhibiting behavior praiseworthy by its close correspondence with my prejudices.

Virulent: adj.:
more robust than I would like it to be.

Virus: n.:
husky, if small, microbe.

Vision: n.:
a hallucination, after its trip to the spin doctor.

Visionary: n.:
1) someone who can have wet dreams without going to sleep.

2) one who has been blinded by his rose-colored glasses.

3) a fanatic with a good press agent.
one who has an unusual ability to sell his hallucinations
    adj.:
impractical, imbecilic or inane.

Voicemail: n.:
the method we use to provide impersonal service.

Volcano: n.:
geological zit.

Volunteer: v.i.:
demonstrate one's lack of military experience.

Volunteerism: n.:
formalization of "let George do it."

Vote: v.i.:
show support at the ballot box for one's political bosses.

Vote of confidence: n.:
a ballot cast in support of the Spanish Prisoner.

VR: acronym:
an activity developed for people who are unable or unwilling to confront actual reality.

Vulgar: adj.:

1) ordinary; popular; pertaining to the man in the street.

2) base; offensive; degraded.
This illustrates the affinity that wordmongers have for the people in the real world.

W

W: initial:
pronounced "Dub-ya." Republican for "minor" or "lesser", euphemistically, "Junior."

Wag: n.:
smartass.

Wage: n.:
the name given the periodic payment made when slaves are rented or leased rather than bought.

Wage slave: n.:
one obtained on the installment plan. Payments may be scheduled weekly, biweekly, semimonthly or monthly, depending on the convenience of the payer. The convenience of the payee is not considered to be relevant.

Walking: n.:
the exercise that replaced running during the greying of America.

Wall Street: n.:
geographic center of America's financial industry.

Its name has given us such evocative images as "back to the wall" and "up against the wall."

"Hitting the wall" is a related idea.

War: n.:
a mechanism used by old men to decrease the competition from young men for available females.

"War is Hell": maxim:
a sentiment attributed to a man who did is utmost to make it a truism.

A vast understatement of war's true worth. Can you imagine GB Shaw writing "Don Juan at War" as a satiric piece?

War on Drugs: n.:
the government's price support program for the narcotics industry.

Warrant: n.:
license to ignore the law.

Warrior: n.:
one who understands the principle "kill them all; God will recognize his own."

Wary: adj.:
paranoid, as in "children are taught to be wary of strangers."

Washington, D.C.: proper name:
the ironic city: named for the man who could not tell a lie, it is the seat of a government that cannot tell the truth.

Watermelon: n.:
a fruit whose very existence is an affront to the Politically Correct.

We: pronoun:
1) I, as in "We can see the success of the Administration's policies."
2) you, as in "We will all have to make sacrifices."

Wealth: n.:
the only consistently effective system of birth control.

Weapon: n.:
a tool, capable of causing injury, that I don't know how to use.
An implement designed to extend a warrior's reach—usually to exceed his grasp.

Weapons of mass destruction: n.:
media name for our most important security assets when held by anyone we disapprove of.
The mechanized wholesalers among the Merchants of Death.

Whiskey: n.:
the refined principle of John Barleycorn.

Whisky: n.:
the life-giving water of the land of the Gaels.

Whistle: v.i.:
play the only musical instrument more portable than a harmonica.

White: adj.:
1) wicked;
2) off-color.

White House: proper name:
exclusive bed-and-breakfast in D.C., operated by and for the National Committee of the party in the Oval Office.

White paper: n.:
a report written using whitewash for ink.

Whitewater: n.:
1) the noisy, flashy way to get back down when you've been up the creek. Dangerous without a paddle.
2) a fluid medium from which Republicans have attempted to formulate a whitewash for a certain edifice from Georgia.

Whitewater investigation: n.:
a political venture in which Republican senators undertake to prove that a former Democrat governor was a lawyer and a politician, and that he had the audacity to act like a Republican governor without benefit of GOP sanction.

Wholistic: adj.:
marketeering term emphasizing the unity of patient's mind and body, patient's pocketbook and doctor's hand.

Wicca: n.:
an ancient and honored naturist society. Most of the key rituals were originally performed without the concealing or misdirecting influence of raiment.

Wildlife: n.:
what parents think their children are experiencing at college; the traditional Greek lifestyle.

Wildlife preserves: n.:
nondomesticated biota protected against loss or spoilage: buffalo jerky,, dried salmon, jellied rattlesnake, things like that.

Wiley: proper name:
author of another dictionary, where the definitions are shorter and the illustrations more profuse. He also writes poetry. Suck rocks, Hart.

Will: n.:
testament to the generosity and pettiness of the human spirit.

Will power: n.:
won't power. No one ever makes an issue of positive accomplishment.

Will o' the Wisp: proper name:
pre-industrial UFO.

Will of the people: n.:
what's left after you've killed their spirit.

Willy: proper name:
nickname for John Thomas. Member of Parliament, stereotypically, an upstanding member; if recently lubricated, a member of the Executive Branch.

Winter: n.:
Mother Nature's naptime.

Wisdom: n.:
1) cleverness tarnished by age.
2) the ability to illuminate, as contrasted with brilliance, the ability to dazzle.

Wise: adj.:
so discerning as to agree with me.

Wit: n.:
twice the usual allotment of cleverness.

Wit and Wisdom: phrase:
a collection of utterances by and cheap shots at a celebrity.
The term is used generously; if it were applied rigorously, most of the "Wit and Wisdom of..." books would be very slim indeed.

Witch hunt: n.:
investigation of my friend; due diligence against my client.

With all deliberate speed: phrase:
with all possible deliberation and very little speed.

Woman: n.:
1) the entity which makes life worth living for a man.
2) the entity which can make life not worth living for a man.

Word: n.:
weapon of the non-violent.

Words: n.:
stumbling blocks in the path to understanding.

Work: n.:
a particularly vicious Anglo-Saxon four-letter word.
"The curse of the drinking class."
"My work fascinates me: I can sit and stare at it for hours."
In another demonstration of the difference between the worlds of science and of everyday life, in physics, work is the ability to change energy (or the result of such a change.) In real life, work only consumes energy.

"Work with a sense of urgency": motto:
work in a constant state of emergency.

Worm: n.:
harvester of Man, beast and higher plants.

Worry: v.i.:
ravel the sleeve of care.

Worship: v.t.:
consider with the same critical assessment as the master his spaniel or the grandmother her grandchild.

Write: v.t.:
participate in a perfectly natural, if somewhat cerebral, activity. If you try it, remember Heinlein's dictum to "do it in private and wash your hands afterwards."

Writer: n.:
an exhibitionist who flaunts his private thoughts and words.

Writing: n.:
"the purpose of writing is to inflate weak ideas, obscure poor reasoning, and inhibit clarity. With a little practice, writing can be an intimidating and impenetrable fog." [Calvin {Bill Watterson}]
According to Heinlein, it's not really something to be ashamed of, but it should be done in private—and wash your hands when you're through.

Wrong: adj.:
in disagreement with me.

Wrongful death: n.:
loss of life of which I do not approve and which may offer an opportunity for profit, if my lawyer talks fast enough.

Wrongful life: n.:
the outcome of a successful anti-capital-punishment demonstration.

X

X: n.:
symbol used to mark an error; as Xmas, Xtian.

X out: v.t.:
typewriter user's equivalent of the Delete key.

X-rated: adj.:
having too much sex and not enough violence to be successful in commercial theaters.

Xanadu: proper name:
capitol of the nation next to Shangri-La.

Xanthippe: proper name:
a classical Greek shrew, whose tongue had such bile as to make hemlock sweet by comparison.

Xenophobia: n.:
the great-grandmother of racism.

Xerox: proper name:
name of the ancient Persian god of paperwork; noted for his dry writing style.

Xylophone: n.:
a musical toy often gifted by grandparents to get revenge on their children.

Y

Yank: v.i.:
>masturbate. It is important to establish whether you will be the yanker or the yankee, though both is common practice.
>
>n.:
>typical foreign honorific for "American", awarded in recognition of their notorious self-sufficiency.

Yard sale: n.:
>grassroots mercantilism.

Ye: article:
>"the." An illiterate affectation by shops that want to appear old-fashioned or "quaint."

Year: n.:
>a period of length 365 days, unless the year's number is divisible by 4, when the length is 366 days, unless the year is divisible by 100, when the length is 365 days, unless the year is divisible by 400, when the length is 366 days, unless the year is divisible by 4000...

Yeast: n.:
polite word for fungus. Possibly the longest domesticated organism, it gives us bread, beer and wine, not to mention a thriving practice of quackery. For the former, we can forgive the last.
that transformative substance which invests pap and yields manna.

Yellow: adj.:
1) the color associated with cowardice.
2) the color associated with journalism.
3) the color considered brightest and most cheerful.

Yellow journalism: n.:
micturochrome reportage.

Yellow Pages: trade mark:
yellow journalism of the directory industry.

Yellow peril: n.:
an image very evocative to a man with prostatitis; enuresis.

Yellow streak: n.:
oriental exhibitionism.

Yes: adv.:
the most dangerous single word in the English language, and the most valuable.

Yew: n.:
a tree used to make Robin Hood's bow for fighting Prince John and for making a magic arrow for fighting breast cancer.

Yippie: n.:
one of a group of left-fringe activists of the 1960s.
There are varying accounts as to the origin of their name: one school holds that they were named for their similarity to the obnoxious "yip-py" little dogs that dowagers and single women go in for; others

maintain it came from their propensity to get stoned and wander around going "Yippee!" at the slightest provocation.

You: pronoun:
1. "You can't be expected to…."

"You can't think straight": phrase:
You don't think like me.

Young: adj.:
invulnerable, omniscient, supremely important, in the eyes of the young.

Youth: n.:
1) a property which the young strive to disguise and the old strive to project.
2) a beatific state wasted on the young; Paradise Lost to the middle-aged; the commodity most squandered by the old in time of war.
3) in Presidential politics, any age below that of retirement.

Yuppie: acronym:
from Young Upward(-ly mobile) Professional. One of a class bearing much the same relation to captains of industry as a remora to a shark.

Z

Zealot: n.:
someone committed to the other side.

Zebra: n.:
a jackass in pinstripes which does not work in an office.

Zen: n.:
a Buddhist sect that teaches that the path to enlightenment is not to strive to find the path to enlightenment.
The Beatniks picked up on the "not to strive" part and left the rest for the Buddhists.

Zero: n.:
nought.
One reason the Government uses budget figures with all those zeros is to show you they've got you by the noughts.

Zero tolerance: motto:
total intolerance.

Ziggurat: n.:
a pyramid rendered in low-resolution graphics.

Zigzag: adj.:
showing the straightforwardness of a political compromise, or a legal decision.

Zinc: n.:
the alternative-medicine wonder drug of the '90s, having edged out selenium. In danger of being displaced by magnesium.
Since the Nixon years, the primary component of copper pennies.

Zionist: n.:
one who denies the humanity of Palestinian arabs.

Zipper: n.:
a post-Victorian mechanical contrivance that allows couples to undress more rapidly.

Zither: n.:
Hippie harp.

Zodiac: n.:
1) the mandala of astrology.

2) a brand of hotrod rubber rafts.

Zombie: n.:
a mixed drink that creates replicas of its namesake. The next morning, you feel a lot as though you had died on a Caribbean island.

Zoo: n.:
1) a place where people go to show off to a captive audience of animals.

2) a municipal replica of the halls of Congress.

Zwieback: n.:
dry milktoast.

Zygote: n.:
chicken to the gamete's egg.